THE LOWDOWN

ERIK CARTER

ISBN: 9781717783493

CHAPTER ONE

New Orleans, Louisiana
The 1970s

HE SAW the black man sitting at the end of the alley, and he knew that he was going to kill him.

A bum. Late forties, maybe fifties. Hunched over. Butt on the ground, back against the wall, head drooped over. It was night, but there was just a tinge of light reaching the man from a lamp on the side of a building farther down the alley. A liquor bottle in a brown paper bag was in the man's left hand. His head moved about, side to side, as though he was in the midst of an animated conversation. But there was no one else in the alley. He was talking to himself.

Just a lousy wino. This would be easy.

Focus. He needed to prepare. He took his attention away from the bum and looked in the rearview mirror. His expression was neutral. He brought the corners of his mouth up. It wasn't quite a smile but rather a look that—once he made his eyes a bit wider, a bit brighter—conveyed openness, naïveté.

He was good at this—the minute changes in appearance

that convinced another person, without saying a word, of one's demeanor, one's character. He was a man full of character and ideals, and he was able to manipulate that sincerity to his will. People responded to it. That's how he'd been able to do what he'd done. No one believed it could be him. No one seemed to remember the simple phrase, *It's always the person you least suspect.*

On the passenger seat beside him was a bag of marijuana, a hand-rolled cigarette, rolling papers, and a small tube of white powder. The marijuana in the bag was laced with cocaine, and the powder was a bit of magic trickery compliments of Dylan Mercer. The key to it all. He put some marijuana onto a paper. Then he opened the tube of Dylan's powder. He raised it over the pot and tapped it with his finger a few times. Way more than was necessary. Dylan had told him to use only a tiny sprinkling. But he had covered the mound of pot in the dust, smiling while he did it. It looked like a small range of snowcapped mountains.

He rolled the joint and put it in his left pocket. He put the cigarette—filled with nothing but pure tobacco—in his right pocket. One more look in the rearview mirror. Minor adjustments to his visage. Pure. Simple. Trustworthy. He stepped out of the car and walked toward the alley.

New Orleans. What a dirty place. Dirty in every sense. Debauchery. Physical filth. It smelled. You could smell the river. And when you were in the French Quarter—the closer you got to Bourbon Street and the strippers and the gays and the alcohol—it smelled like piss. Like human urine. Lingering in the air. A constant assault on the senses.

But this was a different part of the city. Still downtown but far from the French Quarter. There were areas of New Orleans that could get quiet at two in the morning. Quiet and dangerous. But he was willing to accept the danger for what he needed to do. For nights like tonight. This was the fourth or fifth time he'd done this. It was ancillary to the main plan. Hell, it was more than ancillary—it was something different entirely. And if Dylan found out he was doing it again, there'd be hell to pay.

That's why he had to be extra careful.

He checked the stoops as he walked, looking for the mounded form of another bum lying under piles of newspaper or a ratty blanket. But there were none. Perfect. He needed the isolation.

As he drew closer, the bum pulled his head up and looked his way. "You're a long way from home." The bum laughed. A deep laugh. A damned laugh. The laugh of someone clutching a bottle in an alley at two in the morning.

He stepped up beside the bum, a couple feet away. He fought the feelings of revulsion coursing through him. "Yeah, I'm a little bit lost," he said, affecting a voice that matched the trustworthy look on his face. "I'm hoping you can point me toward the French Quarter."

"A tourist." The bum laughed again. He took a drink from his bottle.

"Yep," he said and looked at the ground with a bashful smile. *Aw shucks. Golly, gee whiz.*

"I can help you out," the bum said. "But what's in it for me?"

"I don't have any cash," he said, patting the wallet in his back pocket. "But I have this." He took the joint from his left pocket and held it out.

The bum nodded and took the joint. "My man."

He pulled the clean cigarette from his other pocket, put it in his mouth, and lit it before handing his lighter to the bum.

The bum put the joint in his lips but hesitated before lighting it. "You ain't Jesse James, are you?" He laughed again. An ugly laugh. And loud.

"The outlaw?"

"Nah," the bum said. "Some white guy's been going around lately passing around some real mean stuff. Getcha hooked. People are dying. Bad dude."

"I wrote a check that bounced one time."

More laughter from the bum. He smacked his knee in appreciation. "You're all right." He lit his joint and took a big draw. He sat for a moment, savoring it. "You'd better be careful out here, dressed like you are. All preppy-like. Now to get to the French Quarter, head down to ... down to..."

The bum's eyes grew bigger. Panic set in. A cough. Then a pause. And another cough, louder, harsher. The bum doubled over.

He watched the bum struggle for a moment then flicked his cigarette away down the alley. He took the stupid look off his face.

The bum coughed violently.

He bent down and grabbed the bum by the jacket, pulled him to his feet. He got in the bum's face, gritting his teeth.

Gurgling noises came from the bum's throat. Popping. It was a satisfying sound. Bloody froth came from the corner of the bum's mouth, erupting, spilling down his neck.

"I *am* Jesse James," he said, getting even closer to the bum's disgusting, convulsing face. "Sleep tight, asshole."

He threw the bum aside. The man flopped on the concrete. The bloody foam flowed from his mouth. The movements slowed. Then the bum was still.

He spat on the body and turned toward his car.

CHAPTER TWO

SPECIAL AGENT DALE CONLEY'S back burst into pain as he was thrown against the wall. Two big hands held him by his shirt, lifting him up a couple inches taller than his normal height, putting him eye-to-eye with his assailant.

A big man. No, a gigantic man. As much a beast as a human being. Big jowls covered by a dark, oily, unkempt beard. Long hair full of grease. Small, dull eyes, brown in color. He wore a black leather vest over a stained white tank top. His arms were massive but untoned, echoing the broad chest that was complemented by a massive gut hanging over his heavily soiled blue jeans. Dale liked the look of wear and patina on a pair of 501s, but this man's jeans were nigh destroyed. That in itself was a crime.

The man's name was Bryce.

Dale was in a biker bar on the outskirts of New Orleans. It was called Cast Iron, the type of place that could turn any day into a dank day. Although it was bright and beautiful outside, the sunlight and blazing blue skies hardly permeated the filthy, grime-covered windows. It was dark. Neon lights tossed different colors into the gloom: red, blue, yellow, a splash of purple. There were six pool tables in three rows of two. A bathroom in the back. A few tables in the front on either side of the door. And a bar to the side, behind which the bartender—a man who called himself Sledge and looked like an older version of Bryce—watched the festivities with interest and a wary eye to the underside of the bar, where there was likely a baseball bat or a 12-gauge.

There was a handful of other Bryce-type men scattered around the tables, all of them looking at Dale. Leather pants. Long gray hair. Long white hair. Mustaches. Beards. Body odor. Fat, powerful arms.

And, by himself, on the far wall, was Dale's partner for this assignment, Percy Gordon. Black, mid forties. As always, he was chewing gum. He chewed slowly, a pace that mirrored the cautious, wary look in his eyes that scanned and assessed the tense situation. He sported a mustache and wore an outfit comparable to the other men in the bar.

Dale, too, was wearing a disguise. The 501 jeans and motorcycle boots were his, but he also wore a T-shirt bearing the insignia of Pabst's Blue Ribbon beer and a bulky jean jacket with oil stains and a patch that read, *Ain't We All Got a Mother?*

Dale also had a mustache. A big mustache. Thick and droopy. But unlike Percy's mustache, Dale's was not real. And while Percy's mustache fell straight across his upper lip, Dale had the distinct feeling that his did not. He couldn't see it, of course, but he could sense the adhesive on the left side letting loose of his skin. It felt askew. When the ogre threw him against the wall, it had lost its grip.

Bryce kept his hands on Dale's jacket and drew himself within inches of his face. "You know, usually ringers at pool halls are *better* at pool than they claim to be. But your smart ass strolls in here claiming to have won tournaments, and you haven't sank one goddamn shot."

"Just an off day," Dale said. "I've had a bit of a cold." Dale put his fist to his mouth and let out a little cough. He smiled.

Bryce scoffed, grunted. "Uh-huh. You come to a biker joint in a car like that." He pointed at the murky, dirt-smeared window on the front door, through which was just visible a bright orange sports car. Dale's car. His love. A De Tomaso Pantera. Her name was Arancia. "Some sort of Italian sports car parked right by a bunch of Harleys." He pronounced *Italian* as *Eye-talian*. "You start asking around about Jesse James. And you thought it was a good idea to bring a black guy with you. Into a place like this."

Bryce motioned with his head toward Percy. Dale looked. He and Percy locked eyes. Just for a moment. But they communicated in that moment. *We got this*. Their rapport was near telepathic. This wasn't their first time working together. It was a rarity for Dale to have a second assignment with any of his temporary liaison partners, and this was his *third* with Percy. Which was a blessing. Because Dale liked Percy a lot. They were buddies.

Dale turned back to Bryce.

The big man tightened his grip on Dale's jean jacket. "The only people who come around asking for Jesse James are strung-out addicts and cops. I smell a pig."

Dale held up a finger. "That would be the delicious hot ham and cheese sandwich Sledge prepared for me." He pointed back at the pool table where they had been playing. There was a small table a few feet away where Dale's half-eaten sandwich sat on a paper plate next to a nearly full bottle of beer. Dale hated beer and had mostly feigned drinking it. He looked toward the bar. "*Merci, Monsieur Sledge! Magnifique!*"

The menu at Cast Iron was limited—and it wasn't available in a physical format. Sledge had told Dale and Percy what he could "throw together" for them when they first approached the bar. Given the other options were a hamburger or fried chicken, Dale found the idea of a hot ham and cheese relatively healthy.

Bryce lowered Dale, took one hand off him. "Here's the biggest reason why I know you're full of shit." He tore the mustache off Dale's lip. "Around these parts, guys usually wear *real* mustaches."

Dale put a hand up in a mediating manner. "Listen, I sense a little tension here. I think we started off on the wrong foot. Let's break the ice. I'll start. You can call me Fist." He put out his hand for a handshake.

Bryce gave him a confused look. "Fist?"

"That's right." Dale's extended hand clenched, and he slugged Bryce across the jaw. "Nice to meet you."

Bryce stumbled back several steps before his face snapped back around to Dale. His teeth were bared.

Dale yelled out to his partner. "Let's get the hell out of here, Percy!"

The room erupted into violence. A pool cue came swinging at Dale's head. He dropped down. The cue broke against the wall, a chunk of it falling on his shoulder. Dale popped back up with an uppercut to the man who swung the cue, his fist *thunking* in the man's big belly.

Dale looked across the room.

Percy was surrounded by multiple men, but he was doing a damn good job standing his ground. He kicked one guy in the chest, avoided a roundhouse, then slugged another man across the cheek.

Two more bikers approached. Dale took a swing at one of them, but the man avoided his punch and angled himself around Dale, getting him into a full nelson. The other one pulled back and punched Dale in the stomach, doubling him over. Dale drove his weight down into his heels, propelling himself back up. At the same time he flung his head backwards into the face of the man behind him and then quickly forward into that of the other man. They dropped off him.

Then another man stepped forward.

Bryce.

Nostrils flaring. Ready to explode. Ready to charge. A bull. A raging bull.

Dale considered going for his gun—in the holster clipped to the inside of his jeans against his back—but knew that he didn't have the time. The attack was coming. He positioned himself. Became the matador. Put up his arms.

Ready when you are, toro.

Bryce jumped into action. With perplexing speed given his dimensions, he catapulted himself toward Dale, closing the gap between the two of them in a split second. Dale reached back and grabbed a pool cue by the thin end, swung it like a baseball bat, giving it everything he had. Bryce put up a forearm and snapped the cue, its heavy end flying across the room.

Bryce grabbed Dale by the jacket again, lifted him into the air, and slammed him on his back onto a pool table. He pulled back a big, beefy fist, ready to smash a hole into Dale's face.

People always commented on Dale's ability to improvise.

He needed some of that quick thinking right now.

He looked to his right. Across a field of green felt, there was a multicolored solar system of pool balls.

He grabbed two of the pool balls then quickly sat up and swung his hands together. The two balls cracked against Bryce's skull on either side, into his temples.

The man's eyes went wide, then crossed, then they rolled back in his head. His entire mass crumpled and hit the floor with a tremor that shook the pool table beneath Dale.

Someone else ran up, and an arm with a beer bottle came swinging down toward Dale. He rolled to avoid it, rolling all the way off the opposite side of the table and onto his feet in a crouched position. He scanned his surroundings.

In front of him, there was a clear path to the door. To his right, Percy had also just freed himself for a moment. But a man was coming up behind him.

"Percy!"

Percy turned, saw the other man, and managed to avoid the punch, landing his own blow to the man's jaw.

"Come on!" Dale said.

He ran toward the entrance—with Percy quickly chasing after him—and shouldered his way through the door, which swung back and smacked loudly into the wall. He squinted and covered his eyes. The sunlight was blinding. He reached into the pocket of his jean jacket for his shades as he and Percy ran toward Arancia.

The parking lot was sparse gravel, and stones kicked back from their feet as they ran. There were a half dozen or so bikes, one for each of Cast Iron's patrons, and their chrome metalwork gleamed in the sunlight.

Dale looked back. Behind them, the bikers flooded out of the bar and started toward their bikes.

At the head of the pack, screaming in rage, was Bryce, holding a hand to the side of his head where Dale had cracked him with one of the pool balls. A trickle of blood ran through his fingers.

Dale frantically reached into his pants pocket as he ran toward Arancia. He pulled out his keys. As he and Percy got to the car, he fumbled to get the key into the lock, then jumped in and unlocked the passenger side for Percy.

Dale turned the key in the ignition. Arancia's mighty V8 roared. Dale put the stick into gear and gave it some gas before releasing the clutch. Arancia's tires spun in place, throwing gravel behind her. Dale looked in the rearview.

The bikers covered their heads, darting behind their bikes

as the gravel flew in all directions. Dale could hear the rocks *pinging* off their bikes.

He grinned.

One of the bikers ran up and grabbed Arancia's door handle, right outside the driver's side glass, inches away from Dale.

The man was touching Arancia.

No one touched Arancia.

The tires grabbed hold of solid ground, and Arancia took off. The eyes on the man clinging to her went wide, and he fell to the ground. Dale held on tight to the steering wheel, trying to control the 330-horsepower mass of sheer energy in the unpredictable surface of the gravel parking lot.

They pulled onto the street, and the tires screeched, finally getting something to dig their teeth into. Arancia bolted down the road. Next to Dale, Percy took hold of the dash. The trees and ramshackle buildings of the abandoned side of New Orleans flew by as they sped off.

Percy turned around in his seat. "I don't think our friends were quite ready for us to leave."

Dale flicked his eyes to the mirror. The bikes were all on the road, chasing after them.

"Minor nuisance."

There was a curve ahead. Dale tightened his grip on the wheel and guided Arancia around the curve then dropped the stick another gear and hammered the gas, the inertia throwing his head back.

He looked to the mirror again. The bikes were just now starting to appear around the curve. He'd put some good distance between them.

Another curve in front of them, this one to the left. Dale pulled them through the curve, tires screeching. A few feet ahead there was a crossroad. Dale dropped the stick into a lower gear, and he and Percy jolted forward into their seat belts. He yanked the wheel to the right and exited onto the crossroad.

On the new road, Dale yanked back on the handbrake and turned the wheel. The tires let out a wail. Dale's ears rang. Arancia's whole frame shuddered as she whipped around 180 degrees. Everything was movement, chaos. But it was a controlled chaos. Dale knew what he was doing.

Arancia came to a stop. Her whole mass swayed on her suspension, rocking side to side. Dale was panting. He looked at Percy. His eyes were wide. He too was short of breath.

They had spun all the way around and were now facing the road they had just exited.

"Dale, what is this?"

"Shh," Dale said and put a finger to his lips. He pointed in front of them. "Watch."

A moment later, all of the bikes zipped by. Dale waited a bit, then he casually lowered the handbrake, put Arancia into first gear, and rolled up to the stop sign. He whistled. He turned left, going back the direction from which they had come.

Percy smiled at him. "Well played."

Moments later, they were back where they started. Cast Iron appeared ahead of them on the left. The parking lot was empty save for one bike, baking in the bright sunlight. Sledge's ride, no doubt. As they got closer, Dale slowed down.

And flipped on his turn signal.

Percy started. "What the hell are you doing?"

"Forgot something."

Gravel crunched beneath Arancia's tires as they reentered the parking lot. Dale pulled up beside the bar.

"Dale..."

"Just wait here. Be right back."

Dale stepped out of the car into the bright sunlight and then disappeared into the darkness of Cast Iron once more.

The place was empty. But he knew that Sledge had to be in there. And he also remembered how Sledge had eyeballed the underside of the bar earlier, as though he had some sort of weapon stashed there.

There was the smell of cigarette smoke and sweat. Dale's boots crunched on the debris. He drew his Smith & Wesson and approached the bar.

"Sleeeeeedge? Anybody home?"

Two hands appeared above the surface of the bar. Then the arms. Then Sledge's face. He stood up from behind the bar, arms above his head, hands empty.

"You're one crazy son of a bitch, you know that?" Sledge said in a gravelly voice. "Ain't never had no one clear this whole place out before."

"Step out from behind the bar, Sledge. I don't know what you got back there."

Sledge did as he was asked, keeping his hands above his head as he walked around the bar.

Dale scanned his surroundings. The aftermath of the scuffle was strewn everywhere. Scattered chairs. Upturned tables. Broken beer bottles. But he didn't see it.

"Where is it, Sledge?"

"Where's what?"

Dale's eyes scanned over the detritus ... and then he saw it.

It wasn't where he had left it, but it had somehow escaped the melee. It had even remained on its plate. Dale walked over and grabbed his sandwich. He took a bite and nodded at Sledge, keeping his eyes on him as he backed out of the bar.

"Crazy son of a bitch," Sledge said.

Dale winked.

Through the door, into the sunlight, and back to Arancia's black leather driver's seat. He handed the sandwich to Percy, put Arancia into gear, and took off.

As he stopped at the road before hitting the gas, he saw Percy staring at him. "What?"

Percy didn't reply, just shook his head.

"I paid for the damn thing," Dale said.

"Aren't you going to eat it?"

"I never eat in the car."

Percy looked at the sandwich and back to Dale. "Unbelievable."

CHAPTER THREE

IT WAS ONLY 6 A.M., but still there was a crowd all around Dale. He brought the mug to his lips ... and another person bumped into him. Coffee spilled down the side of the mug onto the saucer.

Percy sat across from him at one of the small tables in the crowded patio area of world-famous Café Du Monde, a spot known for its chicory coffee and beignets. At the start of the assignment, they visited Du Monde on one of their first mornings in New Orleans. After all, it was high on the Big Easy tourist checklist. But as the case dragged on, this was now their third visit. They'd both enjoyed it the first time, so it was a logical place to return to. But the more times they came, the more it reminded Dale that the case was dragging on, getting colder.

The air was thick. It wasn't the most humid time of the year, but even the dead of winter could feel muggy in the Gulf South. Dale once had an assignment in the region in the middle of December. He remembered waking up one morning sweating from the humidity yet feeling cold from the temperature. It was an odd and discomforting sensation.

Café Du Monde sat on Decatur Street, catty-cornered from Jackson Square and a few yards from the Mississippi River. The main patio area was covered in a large awning with its celebrated green and white stripes. There were small round tables with round chairs, each having a napkin dispenser and a jar of sugar. And everywhere there were people. Sweaty tourists. Packed in on themselves.

Dale took a sip of the coffee. The chicory added a certain something to the flavor, sort of a chocolatey effect. He'd passed on getting beignets—a French doughnut served under a mound of powdered sugar. Naturally it didn't jive with Dale's clean lifestyle to eat them very often, and the one time that he did try them—on their first visit to Café Du Monde —he'd failed miserably at eating the things without getting powdered sugar all over himself. Luckily he'd been wearing a white T-shirt that day, so he hadn't ended up looking like a total jerk.

Percy did have a plate of beignets in front of him that morning, and he was doing the smart thing of eating them with a fork. He was careful to keep the powdered sugar off his suit. Dale wore a T-shirt and jeans. Spread on the table in front of the agents were the contents of the case file. Notes. Forms. Gruesome pictures of people lying on the ground, eyes open, frothy blood coming from their mouths.

Percy put down his fork and took a sip of coffee. "Nearly two weeks now since you made case determination, and we're still no further along than when we started."

Dale made eye contact with one of the waitresses across the café. Blonde, on the short side, bright baby blues. She gave him a toothy grin before continuing her conversation with her table. Dale returned his attention to Percy. "So what are you saying?"

"I'm saying that I don't know that this is a case suited to the Bureau of Esoteric Investigation."

"Like you said, I already made the determination."

"But I can always use the reciprocity clause and take the lead."

Dale put his hand to his chest, and, seeing that he was in New Orleans, he used his best Southern belle accent to say, "You wouldn't do a thing like that to little ol' me, now would ya?"

"Face it, Dale. This is a standard DEA matter. If I need help with the racial aspect, I can go to the FBI. The fact that our guy's been calling himself Jesse James is irrelevant."

Dale leaned forward, got more serious. "It *is* relevant. Jesse James was more than just an outlaw. He was a Confederate operative. And nearly all of the people who've died from our Jesse James' funky drugs have been black."

Percy shook his head. "There are a lot of these kind of hateful groups down here. 'The South will rise again.' 'Lincoln was a rotten bastard.'"

Dale felt eyes upon him. The waitress was looking his way. She smiled again. A bit of the early morning light sparkled in her eye. Lovely. Dale smiled back.

Percy snapped his fingers. "Stay with me, Dale. Jesus."

"You're right, pal," Dale said and leaned back in his chair. "There are a lot of groups like that. And we have people dying from tainted drugs in four cities along the coast, from here to Pensacola, Florida. Assuming that these primarily black drug deaths are the coordinated work of one of those hate-based groups, and the only lead we got is a guy who distributes these drugs under the name of a historical figure connected to the Confederacy, you don't think having an expert at solving historical mysteries is a good thing?"

Percy sighed. "So you're telling me this has nothing to do with the fact that I'll be leaving D.C. after this assignment, that this is our last time working together?"

Of course Dale had already considered the fact that this

would be the last chance to spend time with Percy. But hearing him say it made it sting a bit more. They'd formed a friendship in the years since Dale became an agent with the BEI. This covert agency of the Department of Justice tasked Dale with solving crimes in his particular area of specialized knowledge—history and puzzles—pairing him with a different liaison agent for each case. His third assignment, only a couple months into the job, saw him seeking out a network of heroin distribution hidden under the guise of underwater archaeology. It had been a life-changing time for Dale, this third assignment, as he met not only DEA Special Agent Percy Gordon but also treasure hunters Ronan and Al Blair. As fate would have it, Percy and Al Blair ended up being two of the most formative people in Dale's life.

After that first assignment together, Dale got to know Percy away from matters of law enforcement. Percy invited him into his home, and Dale became a family friend. Before he joined the BEI and took his new name, Dale's PI—his prior identity—had never been a family friend to anyone. Getting his new identity had been a fresh start for Dale. He was able to become a whole new person. A better person. A better man. And a big part of that transformation had been the love he was shown by Percy and his family.

Thus, it was entirely feasible that Percy was right, and Dale was clinging to this case for personal reasons. So Dale thought for a long, hard moment about it. Was he *really* sure that this was a BEI case? Was he deluding himself? Could it be that he was selfishly pulling his talents away from other cases where they might be better utilized?

But then he thought about the Jesse James connection. And he knew he was onto something. "The historical Jesse James was a bushwhacker. A guerrilla combatant for the CSA. There's something to that. I know there is. I genuinely think this is a BEI case. Besides, don't flatter yourself. If I was stalling, it would only be because I haven't gotten to go to the beach yet."

Percy finished his last beignet. He took a napkin from the dispenser and wiped his mustache clean of powdered sugar. "Dale, we're friends. When my family and I move to Houston, that's not going to change. We don't see each other that often as it is."

Dale was getting uncomfortable. He wanted to avoid the topic, and Percy was getting borderline touchy-feely. Dale hated touchy-feely. He diverted the conversation. "And is the family prepared for the move?"

"Bonita's ready for a change, but she's gonna miss her folks, of course. Jeanne has a few little friends she's torn about leaving. But she's seven. She'll be fine. I'm most worried about leaving Erv at Georgetown by himself."

Dale still couldn't believe Ervin was a full-fledged college student. In Dale's mind, Ervin would always be a high school kid. "Sophomore year. I'm sure he's well adapted by now."

Percy looked away. "It's his second year, but he's a freshman by credits. Failed some classes. Spending all his time with this crowd of his."

Dale knew that there had been bad blood between Percy and Ervin in the last year or so, and while he didn't want to talk about any more touchy-feely, he'd be an ass if he didn't acknowledge it. So he said, "You two doing any better?"

"He hates me. More than your average teenager hates his father. He hates that I work for the DEA. He smokes grass, rubs it in my face. He hates that I work with white folk. Hates you, if truth be told."

"Hmph!" Dale said, feigning indignation once more. "And I gave that kid pointers on women."

Percy frowned. "He's in some sort of protest group. Won't admit to it, but I know that he is. From what I've heard, they seem violent. I couldn't handle it if he got involved in something. If he hurt someone. Or himself. I just don't know what to do with the boy."

"Ervin's nineteen years old, partner. He's not a boy. He's a young man, and he's gotta figure all this out for himself."

"He'll always be my boy." Percy exhaled, paused, then drained the rest of his coffee. He reached into his pocket, unwrapped a piece of gum, and popped it in his mouth. He offered a slice to Dale, who declined. "And the sooner I can get this case completed, the sooner I can get some quality time with him before classes start again. So if you'll just please concede that this isn't a BEI case, I can take full control of the task force and move forward with this."

The waitress walked across the patio, and Dale saw a glimmer from her left hand. It was a wedding band. A smile tease, that's what this girl was. Foul temptress.

Dale put his hands behind his head and took a deep breath. "This *is* a BEI case, Percy. I know it. Listen, I've got one more good lead for us. Let me follow up on that. If it doesn't pan out, use the reciprocity clause, and the case is all yours."

"The Grizzly?"

Dale nodded and flipped through the papers on the table. "I got an address. This guy's got his hands in pot, coke, prostitution. He only meets by appointment, so I guess we'll have to start off on the wrong foot with him. But, hey, with a name like Grizzly, what could possibly go wrong?"

CHAPTER FOUR

JESSE RICHTER STOOD on a dirt path in a field of grass surrounded by forest. The grass was halfway up his shin. The sun was bright. The property was large and stretched out in front of him. In the back, about a hundred yards away, was a large pole barn, its metal siding painted dark brown. A few feet in front of him was a trailer home.

It wasn't dilapidated, but it was in need of attention. Some paint, a little rust repair. It was gray at the top, white on the bottom, with a couple blue accent designs. A small wooden awning had been built over the front door. The awning's top was a piece of corrugated polycarbonate, and it covered a small stoop with a thin metal railing and three steps leading down to the ground. There were two windows to the left of the door, and to the right was a larger set of windows for the trailer's living room area. These were cracked open. A window unit air conditioner jutted out of the right side of the trailer, and there was a smaller one on the opposite side, that being for the bedroom of Dylan and his wife, Luanne, Jesse's cousin. Neither A/C unit was running. There was silence from the trailer. Jesse heard only the birds in the trees.

He stared at the trailer, waiting on Dylan Mercer. Jesse knew why he'd been summoned here, why he'd been told to make the three-hour drive from New Orleans to the country near Cantonment, Florida. Dylan had gotten word of what had happened the previous evening. He knew that Jesse had gone off script, that he'd killed another bum.

That's why Jesse had been waiting so long. Almost five minutes now. In the Florida sun and humidity. Sweating. The sunlight burning his scalp. Dylan was making him feel the anticipation. Jesse himself had a knack for theatrics, so he understood what Dylan was trying to accomplish when he did things like this. This objective analysis did make Dylan's theatrics seem more benign, but still Jesse couldn't separate himself entirely from his gut, emotional reaction.

The truth was, Jesse was anxious. About what Dylan was going to do with him.

The door opened. Halfway. Paused. Then it swung open entirely, and out walked Dylan Mercer. He was long. Six foot three with loping arms and thin legs. He wasn't from the South, but he nonetheless reminded Jesse of boys he'd grown up with in Mississippi. His face had that same lean, wild look, and his beard said *I don't give a shit*, growing unrestrained down his neck, spattered with gray hairs. He wore a faded black T-shirt with white paint stains and a tear across the side. Jeans. Boots.

Dylan looked at Jesse. Waited a moment. Then descended the stairs, lighting a cigarette as he approached. He maintained eye contact with Jesse as he walked up to him. He stopped a couple feet from him, looked him up and down. Laughed. "You worthless fool." His words oozed contempt in that Northern accent of his. He'd laughed, but Dylan was far from joking. There was that darkness in his eyes. "So ... Jesse just had to kill himself another Negro."

"I didn't think anyone would see," Jesse said. He knew Dylan hated excuses, but it was all Jesse could think to say.

"You didn't think a soul was in those buildings surrounding you?" Dylan blew smoke out the corner of his mouth. The smell of tobacco filled Jesse's nose.

"It ... Nothing happened the other times." Jesse avoided Dylan's eyes. He looked to the ground and back up. Found him staring at him still.

Dylan took a long drag off his cigarette and leaned his head back as he assessed Jesse. "It's your fault we're in this predicament. Calling yourself Jesse James. Couldn't leave it at that, could you? You ignorant pile of shit."

That accent. Northern. Jesse despised it. Especially when Dylan was lecturing him, talking down to him like this. It was a Midwestern accent. Neutral. Like people on TV. Like a teacher, like the professors from Jesse's days at LSU. Dylan used it with such contempt. As much as Dylan fit in down here in the South, as accepted as he was—his leadership of this organization being the ultimate proof of such acceptance —he always had a foot in the North. This gave Jesse a degree of distrust. Even though he was following him into this holy war. Even though they were kin by marriage.

Jesse hated apologizing to people. He hated lowering himself like that. But he reminded himself again of his need to remain humble if he was going to be a productive part of the team. "I'm sorry."

Dylan scoffed. "Our investors have sunk a fortune in this. We got all these other guys involved. And you're out there taking chances with it all."

"I just ... get so damn angry."

"No. You're being foolish. And if you put this in jeopardy one more time, I'll deal with you personally. I think you know what that means." Dylan stared into him for a moment. "Have you found the symbol?"

He flicked his cigarette into Jesse's chest. Jesse felt the heat of its tip for a split second before it dropped to the ground. Dylan turned toward to the trailer before giving Jesse a chance to answer his question.

Jesse stayed where he was. Dylan didn't want him to follow, just to answer. "It's supposed to be in one of the Saint Louis Cemeteries. Some sort of moon shape on a tomb. I looked all afternoon. There are so many moons. And three different cemeteries. Hundreds of tombs. I need more details."

Dylan stopped on the trailer's small front porch. He put his hands on the metal railing and looked back at Jesse. "Excuses."

"I can find this symbol, Dylan. I promise you."

"You sure as hell better hope you do." He stepped into the trailer. The door snapped shut behind him.

CHAPTER FIVE

DALE AND PERCY looked at the alley. The sky was gray and gloomy, and they were in an equally gloomy area of New Orleans. The alley was strewn with debris, but there was a clear path down the center, which was exactly what Dale needed. It was angled down a steep slope. And there was a straight shot to the dumpster.

Dale grasped the handle of a battered shopping cart. It was filled with four cinderblocks that Dale had found nearby.

Percy looked at him skeptically, slowly chewing his gum. "What the hell are you up to now, Dale?"

"Some very delicate police work."

Dale let loose of the cart. It rolled quickly down the hill into the alley.

"Come on!" Dale said.

He darted off to the front of the brick building to which the alley belonged. Percy followed. As they reached the front of the building, Dale came to an abrupt stop, then assumed a casual stroll as they rounded the corner.

A few feet ahead of them was an unassuming and unmarked door. There were windows covered by boards, painted black, as was the rest of the front of the building. By the door was a guard wearing a black suit with a black shirt and white tie. He was thick and wide, sported a beard, and he wore sunglasses even in the murky weather. His head was a small boulder, both in size and shape.

A metallic crashing noise came from the alley in the back. The shopping cart had found its mark. Dale suppressed a smile, feeling very impressed by his own cleverness.

The guard snapped to attention. He darted off and disappeared beyond the opposite corner of the building—a side alley leading to the wider alley in the back.

Dale nodded at Percy, and they hurried to the the door and went inside.

Every eye in the room fell upon them. Everyone stopped moving. And they stared. It wasn't totally unlike when the two of them first crossed the threshold of Cast Iron.

Dale gave a cheesy grin to his new friends and took in his surroundings. It was a single room. Tables. People playing dice. Several poker games. A roulette table. Men with beers. Women in lingerie and tall boots. Aside from a harried man in the back with his sleeves rolled up and his tie loosened, Dale was the only white face.

And he and Percy were the only two who looked like they lived on the law-abiding side of the tracks.

The walls were painted black, which along with the low lighting coming from the few fixtures hanging from the ceiling, gave the place a very dark and somewhat ominous look. The metal support beams were painted white, and there were little touches of dark red here and there: along the edge of the bar in the back, the bathroom door frames. Dale was impressed that some thought had been given to the interior design of the place.

Dale shut the door as the two of them entered, sealing out what exterior light was coming in and making the place even darker. All those contentious eyes watched them. Another guard approached from the back. He wore the same outfit as the outside guard—a black suit and shirt with white tie. He too wore sunglasses, his resting over a set of massive sideburns. This man was even bigger than the first. And he was a leaner type of big. Pure muscle. Long arms, long face, jutting cheekbones.

As the man approached, Dale leaned over to Percy and said quietly, "Now, just play it cool. A little diplomacy will go a long way here."

"I'm cool."

The guard stepped up within a few feet of them. Towering, peering down. He wore a grin. An aggressive grin. "You lost, fellas?"

"We'd like a word with the Grizzly," Dale said.

"Got an appointment?"

Percy took out his badge. "Indeed we do."

Dale turned to him. "Very diplomatic."

The guard barely acknowledged the badge. He laughed. "DEA. Wrong address. Your appointment's somewhere else. On the other side of town. Dig?"

The front door burst open. The outside guard rushed in, panting. He approached them.

The bigger man with the sideburns gave the other an antagonistic look. "Hell of a job watching the door, Mickey."

Mickey stood tall, straightened his tie, caught his breath. "Is there a problem here?"

Sideburns looked at Dale and Percy as he answered. "Just a couple lost little piggies."

"As I was telling your associate," Dale said to Mickey, "we're here to see the Griz."

Mickey didn't crack a smile. "Don't call him that. You got a warrant?"

"Should we go get one?" Dale said. "I see plenty of illegal

gambling."

Sideburns cocked his head. "See, this here is private property. And you weren't invited. That's trespassing. And ... what's that? Did you just make an inappropriate pass at one of the girls?"

"Haven't had a chance yet," Dale said.

Mickey nodded, seeing where Sideburns was going. "You can't touch her like that. Now we got every right to lay hands on you."

It happened instantly. The guards pounced on Dale and Percy, one attacking each of them. Sideburns came at Dale, clipping him on the chin. Dale staggered backwards and ran into someone. He turned around, fists drawn, and found that it was Percy he'd bumped into. His fists were drawn too and ready to slug Dale. Both men turned back around.

Dale threw a punch into Sideburns' face. Barely made a dent. The man smirked it off. Then he put two big hands on Dale and threw him to the side. Dale crashed into a table, its edge digging into his side. Cards went flying. People screamed, ran for the door. Dale slid off the edge of the table and onto the floor. Sideburns lumbered over to him, and Dale pulled back his right leg, wound it tight, ready to explode his boot into the man's sternum. He saw exactly where he was going to kick him. Just below the neck. Like he was looking down a sight, a scope.

Then there was a noise from the back of the room. A voice.

"What the hell is going on out here?"

It was a low voice, a grumbling voice. Like a storm ready to let loose of its lightning or the primordial growl of one of the alligators in the nearby bayous.

But when Dale looked to see where the voice had come from, it wasn't a gator.

It was a Grizzly.

CHAPTER SIX

Percy Gordon looked around the office and quickly realized one thing about the Grizzly: the man liked chess.

Everywhere were chess pieces: bishops on the bookshelves to the side, a couple knights by the window, a three-foot-tall rook ashtray beside the desk. On the floor was a shag rug of alternating black and white squares. Percy counted the squares—eight-by-eight, white in right. Chess sets of marble. Metal. Wood. Oversized chess sets. Palm-sized chess sets. The back wall was painted black with a line of large, white silhouettes of the six chess pieces: a pawn on the left side and finishing with a king on the right. The surface of the Grizzly's desk, too, was a chessboard, and the four legs holding it aloft were rooks. Dwarfing everything, in each of the back corners of the room, were a gigantic, ceiling-height king and queen.

The Grizzly was behind the desk, seated in a chair that was styled a bit like a throne with its red velvet cushions and polished brass metalwork. Unlike most thrones, however, it reclined, and the springs beneath the cushion squeaked under the Grizzly's girth. This king liked comfort.

He was even bigger than his guards, but he didn't have the

same look of physical power that they had. It was a different sort of power he exuded. The power of influence. You took one look at the guy and knew he was the type of man who got things done. Even with his ridiculous outfit. A green suit. Dark, hunter green. The cuffs and the trim above the pockets were maroon velvet as was the band that went around his fedora hat, which matched the dark green of his suit. He wore sunglasses like his goons. There was no shirt under his jacket, and his bare chest was covered in thick hair reminiscent of his moniker.

Percy and Dale sat across from him in the two chairs facing the desk. He'd been generous enough to give them each an ice pack, which they were both applying to their fresh bumps and bruises.

Percy glanced beside him. Dale was stretching the fingers on his right hand. His knuckles were pinked. There was a scratch on his cheek. And he was grinning. Ear to ear. He enjoyed stuff like this. The fool actually enjoyed getting into fights, being whisked away to foreboding offices to meet criminal bosses. Some people were thrill-chasers. But not Dale. Thrills chased him.

There was something else there, though. Something in Dale's eyes. Almost a bit of reluctance. Distrust, perhaps. Percy felt it too. It was strange, his being a DEA agent and willingly sitting in a drug lord's office. It felt wrong. And it made him tense. He was smashing his chewing gum between his teeth. He took a deep breath, tried to relax.

The Grizzly looked across his desk at the two agents, a hand to his chin. Still smiling. He had been smiling when he first broke up the fight, and he hadn't stopped. Percy felt like a guard at a lunatic asylum. Why was everyone but him smiling? This was not a smiling occasion.

"So, you two come into my establishment, mess with my

guards, and tear the place up. And now you want information out of me?"

"That's correct," Percy said.

The Grizzly laughed, a deep, hearty laugh that matched his voice. "You two got balls. I'll give you that. But I fail to see how talking to you is going to benefit me."

Dale leaned forward. "The guy we're after is killing off some of your best clients."

"You're looking for Jesse James."

Dale nodded.

The Grizzly's smile brightened. "I thought that might be what this is about. Still, I don't see why I should help." He pointed at Percy. "This guy's DEA!"

The Grizzly was right that every inch of Percy wanted to haul the big man off to prison. When you're trained to hunt down scumbags, it was hard to willingly let one go. But Percy had been in enough situations like this to know that getting the help of one scumbag could lead to taking down even bigger scumbags.

Percy shook his head. "I'm not saying I'm going to forget what I've seen or heard about you, but for right now, we're on the same side. And it's in your best interest to help us."

The Grizzly put his fingers together and rested them under his nose. "Well, you're right. Jesse James has been a fly in my ointment." He paused. "His shit's laced. With coke. That's why all the junkies are getting hooked."

"Hooked, yes," Percy said. "But only some of them are dying."

The Grizzly shrugged. "Maybe they're ODing. I don't know."

"They're not overdosing," Dale said in a serious tone. "They're being poisoned. Traces of a chemical has been found in their blood. Similar to arsenic. And not just here. In Biloxi, Mobile, and Pensacola too. That's a two-hundred-mile stretch of death. The only lead we have is this Jesse James, seems to be the ringleader here in New Orleans. We need to know what he looks like."

The Grizzly gave Dale a respectful nod, clearly impressed by his passion. As irreverent as Dale acted sometimes, his motivations were completely pure. He was one of the most genuine people Percy had ever met.

"Poisoned..." the Grizzly said, his smile disappearing as he weighed the gravity of what Dale had said. "He's white. blond. That's all I know. They say he comes and goes. Like a shadow. A ghost. An angel of death."

"Why do it?" Percy said. "If he's dealing, why put stuff out there that's gonna kill his clients?"

"Tell ya the truth, I'm thinking this Jesse James business is about more than drugs. I'm thinking it's some kind a quest. Like a mission or something."

In his time as a DEA agent, Percy had heard a lot of excuses for dealing drugs, but he'd never heard of anyone being on a mission before.

Dale looked at Percy and then back at the Grizzly. "A mission? Why do you say that?"

"Rumor has it he's out searching for symbols. And if he is, he's come to the right place." The Grizzly laughed. The smile returned. "New Orleans is full of them." He strummed his fingers on the desk and looked at them for a long moment. Behind his smile, his mind was debating something. "Here. Take this."

He opened a drawer and took out a plastic bag. It was clear, about the size of a sheet of paper, and there was a bit of pot settled at the bottom. He handed it to Dale.

"One of my guys was out dealing. Saw a competitor selling some shit. The guy he sold it to keels over, has a seizure or something. My guy chases the dealer down. Couldn't catch him. But he dropped that bag. Maybe you can get something out of the residue."

Dale looked at the bag. "We very well might. The dealer your guy chased down—Jesse James?"

"No. This guy was white, but he wasn't blond. Everyone who claims to have seen Jesse James talks about his bright blond hair."

"Why haven't you told any of this to the police?" Percy said.

"I am right now, aren't I?"

The smile grew larger.

The Grizzly was starting to annoy Percy. He was playing mind games with him and Dale. A chess game. But Percy didn't have time for games. He needed answers.

"We're going to need more cooperation out of you," Percy said.

"Haven't I given enough?"

Percy kept his eyes locked on him. He wasn't going to back down. "If you find out anything else, you just let us know. Hear?"

The Grizzly didn't look away either. He kept smiling. Finally he said, "I'll do that."

There was a tapping on Percy's shoulder. It was Dale, giving him a look that said, *Let's get out of here while we're ahead.* Dale stood up. Percy followed suit.

"Thanks for your time, Mr. Bear," Dale said.

CHAPTER SEVEN

As Dale walked with Percy down the street and away from the entrance to the Grizzly's club, he fought the urge to run back, kick in the door, and start making arrests.

So many people there who needed arresting.

Though he appreciated the Grizzly's cooperation, Dale hated being in the situation in which he'd currently found himself—asking a known criminal for assistance. It wasn't the first time he'd had to do something like this during his time as an agent, and he despised turning a blind eye to crime for the sake of doing justice to some greater crime.

He didn't like the idea of trivializing crime for any reason at all, and it bothered him that the public seemed so willing to do so—heist movies and the like, stories that glamorized criminals. In a movie or a novel, a bank heist could be a farcical romp. In reality, there would be collateral damage to the innocent. Every single time. At a minimum, innocent people would be frightened for their lives. The people in the bank—the tellers, the customers. There was not a damn thing that was cute about a bank heist. Even more disturbing was the fact that society had glamorized *actual* violent criminals—

people like Prohibition-era mobsters and Bonnie and Clyde. The truth was, Bonnie and Clyde had ended people's lives. Ruthlessly. Both police and civilians. Real people.

So Dale would get the information he needed out of the Grizzly, but he wouldn't forget what the man stood for.

They approached Arancia, who was parked along the side street from where they'd launched the shopping cart. Dale had been worried about leaving her alone in this rough neighborhood. There were a couple guys eyeballing her as he and Percy approached. They walked away.

When they got to the car, Dale held the bag he'd gotten from the Grizzly up to the sky. It was still overcast, but there was plenty of light. There were crumbles in the bottom of the baggie, dust coating the interior surface.

Percy leaned over. "We'll definitely be able to get something out of that residue, but even if the same chemical is present, it proves nothing, just that the drugs were in there. There might be some prints, but any number of the Grizzly's people have touched and contaminated it."

Dale noticed something. Markings at the top of the bag. "Wait a minute. There's something here."

The marks were small. Scratchy. But definitely deliberate.

Dale quickly unlocked Arancia's door and popped the hood. Since a Pantera was a rear-engine machine, the trunk was in the front not the back. He found the black canvas bag he kept there and took out his magnifying glass.

Percy chuckled. "You bring that thing around with you? Who are you, Sherlock Holmes?"

Dale ignored him. He examined the marks under the glass. They were in the upper right-hand corner, a slash mark and a twisted G.

There was a similar marking at the bottom of the bag, a slash with a dot, in the lower right-hand corner.

"Jackpot!"

Dale's eyes lit up. Seeing the markings made his inner historian go berserk. They were symbols of some sort. He had no doubt in his mind. And he recognized them—but he couldn't recall from where.

He was bouncing with energy as he handed the magnifying glass to Percy. "Take a look at these marks."

Percy squinted at the glass. "I don't know. Could be part of the manufacturing process."

"No, look how the plastic is melted a bit. Those marks have been put there after the fact, pressed in with a hot form."

Percy nodded. "You're right. I see the scoring. Just a hint of brown around the edges. And they look handwritten." He handed the glass and bag back to Dale. "But this could be some random bag the dealer picked up. Those scratches aren't a connection with Jesse James' tainted drugs."

"They are if we find more of those markings in the future."

"And the historical connection? The reason you're staying on this case?"

"Don't you see? They're not just markings. They're symbols. The Grizzly just told us that Jesse James is going around New Orleans looking for symbols." Dale tapped the corner of the bag. "And I know I've seen these symbols before. Somewhere..."

He looked to the ground, thinking deep and hard. Where the hell had he seen them?

Percy shoved his hands in his pockets, chewed his gum slowly, deliberately, assessing Dale for a moment. "All right, Dale. A little longer. But we need to figure out if those really are historic symbols. You know who knows a few things about symbols?

"Who's that?" Dale said with a measure of patience. He knew exactly who Percy was talking about. And it frustrated him that Percy was even mentioning the person.

"Al, of course."

"Yes. Al Blair. Of course," Dale said and rolled his eyes. "I don't need Al's help on this. But thanks for the vote of confidence."

CHAPTER EIGHT

THE GRIZZLY PUSHED through the door and stepped onto the roof of the building. Rhino—his favorite guard, he of the massive arms and even more massive sideburns—followed him. There was a just a bit of chill to the air, and the Grizzly pulled his coat tighter.

He should have been furious. The two agents had come uninvited and torn his place all to hell. But they had guts. He admired that. And while he'd never been one to cooperate with the fuzz, he'd also never come across anyone like Jesse James—haunting the streets, killing silently. The Grizzly sure didn't want to see people dying.

Especially potential clients.

He walked up to the edge of the building. Rhino stepped beside him. Below, he saw the two feds standing beside a bright orange sports car. Looked Italian.

"Nice ride," Rhino said.

The Grizzly grunted.

The agents were in the middle of a conversation. Something serious. Analyzing the information and evidence that he'd given them, no doubt.

Rhino ran a hand across his chin, contemplating. "This is trouble."

The Grizzly watched the agents for a few moments before he responded. Their intense conversation concluded and they got in the car. "You might be right."

"Do you trust them?"

The car started, a roar from what must have been a massive engine.

"No, I don't," the Grizzly said as he watched the car disappear down the street. "That's why you're gonna follow them."

CHAPTER NINE

DYLAN MERCER SAT at the small desk facing the window that looked toward the back side of his property where the pole barn sat. He was in the trailer's master bedroom. Wood paneling covered the walls. Behind him was a queen-sized bed covered in a blue-and-white quilt Luanne's mother had made. Beyond that was a dresser. It was twilight outside, and the scene before him was lit by a light pink sky. A phone receiver was pressed between Dylan's ear and his shoulder, and as he listened to the voice on the other line, he watched the men parking their cars and entering his barn. Most had already arrived, but a few were trickling in. The guest of honor had yet to arrive. This troubled Dylan.

Mick Henderson had been speaking for a while now. Dylan had met him in person a few times, so he'd gotten a good feel for the man's temperament—business-casual, slightly jovial, and never downbeat. But now there was palpable concern in Henderson's voice. He was losing faith in the operation.

"And you can assure us that more will be delivered?" Henderson said in his Southern accent.

"Two hundred more pounds will be distributed tomorrow," Dylan said. "Not a thing to be concerned about, Henderson. Our operation won't be compromised because of one man's incompetence. We have several more recruits. In fact, one is just about to be indoctrinated. I won't let this fail because of Jesse Richter. He's a good knight. He just needs to be reigned in."

Henderson exhaled. "I'll pass the info on to the other investors, but that's not going to be enough to put their minds at ease. I've been asked to inform you that we're meeting with you. Tomorrow."

For a moment, Dylan couldn't respond. This wasn't the arrangement that had been agreed upon. The investors wanted to remain faceless. Unseen. Unknown.

Dylan took in a frustrated breath and fought the urge to lash out. He despised being told what to do. But he knew that the whole of the operation rested on the investors' input. Their millions of dollars. They had him by the short hairs. So, like a subservient wretch, he managed to say, "Absolutely. In person?"

"That's right," Henderson said. "In person and in public."

"If that's what they want."

"I'm getting nervous too, Dylan," Henderson said, his tone darkening even more. "I don't trust Jesse Richter. He's jeopardizing our side venture."

"I can handle Jesse. We only need him to find the last symbol in New Orleans. After that, we're in the clear."

"I hope you're right."

The other line went dead. Dylan hung up the phone.

Outside, a new vehicle arrived at the barn. A pickup truck. It came up beside the building—nearer to the door than the other vehicles—and stopped. Jesse Richter got out of the driver's side and walked to the passenger door. He had a shit-eating grin on his face. He pulled another man from the passenger seat. Blindfolded. Hands tied behind his back. The man was blond like Jesse. Jesse had chosen several blond recruits. More of his single-mindedness, the kind of simple thinking that was putting the whole operation in jeopardy.

Dylan got up from the desk. There was a chest in the corner of the room that he kept padlocked. He knelt down and unlocked it. Sitting on top of the pile within was a knight's helmet. He'd had the helmet—and all the subsequent helmets—crafted exactly as they were described in the historical document: topped with red and white feathers with a visor of metallic plates.

He stood up and held the helmet in front of him. He ran a hand over the feathers, and a bemused smile came to his lips. It all seemed so theatrical, so over-the-top. But these Southern hillbillies ate it up. Being part of the organization, wearing the ridiculous outfit during nights like tonight—it gave the idiots a sense of purpose, a sense that they were part of something.

Dylan would happily provide it to them.

————

It was almost completely dark outside by the time Dylan approached the pole barn. He put his helmet on and pulled open the sliding door. There were about a dozen men, all dressed as he was: wearing chainmail and the helmets with red and white feathers. They were arranged in a semicircle, and a couple of the men held flaming torches, casting an eerie glow into the darkness of the barn, throwing shadows onto the walls. All of the knights' swords were drawn and angled down into a convergence at the center of the semicircle. This was where the blindfolded man was, on his hands and knees, kneeling on a mass. He was shirtless now, and there were bloody spots all over him where the swords' tips had pierced his skin. He shivered violently. His right hand was on a Bible. His left hand was directly on the mass beneath him.

The knights turned to look at Dylan. They kept their swords pointed at the shaking man.

Dylan walked toward the group. As he did, he could see Jesse Richter to the right. He was dressed identically to everyone else, of course, but Dylan knew it was him. He could tell it by the energy, the arrogance that was evident in his poise, his demeanor even when covered with twenty pounds of metal. Jesse was a problem. He was this operation's greatest soldier—but he was also its greatest liability.

And, if Dylan didn't control him, Jesse could very well be their undoing.

Dylan stopped when he reached the man on the ground. He drew his sword. It made a satisfying noise as it left his scabbard, like something from a movie. The sound made the man shake even more than he had been. Dylan leveled his sword at the man and nicked his chest with the razor-sharp tip. The man yelled out.

This made Dylan question the recruit's resolve. If he was this frightened already, wait until he saw what he was kneeling on.

Dylan spoke. "Those who would pass here must face both fire and steel. Are you willing to do so?" They were the exact words that had been spoken so many years ago. Pulled directly from the document. Word for word.

The man was so frightened that Dylan could hardly hear his response. "I am."

"And you solemnly swear to support this organization such that the South will rise again?"

"I do."

Dylan dropped his tone a bit, tried to be even more ominous. "The penalty for breaking this oath: quartering, your body cast out to the east, north, west, and south." He paused. "The penalty is *death*."

Dylan pulled the blindfold off the man, and someone in the back threw on the barn's overhead lights, flooding the space with brightness. The man squinted.

The two knights on either side of the man released his arms, and he looked down at what his hands had been resting upon. Under his right hand had been a Bible. Underneath his left hand was a face. The corpse of a black man. One of the victims of Dylan's drugs.

The man shrieked. He scuttled away and saw what he had been kneeling on—the body of another black man.

The knights begin to chant.

"Death! Death! *Death!*"

The man continued to scream, his wails echoing off the barn walls.

CHAPTER TEN

DALE PUSHED the empty bowl of jambalaya away across the table. He put a hand on his full stomach. Cajun food rocked.

The cuisine was enough of a reason to visit New Orleans, but there was so much more that Dale loved about the place. He wasn't particularly keen on large cities, so it was odd that New Orleans had ended up as one of his favorite places. He had been there once before this assignment and knew then that he had to some day return. It had been truly a case of leaving one's heart behind in a city. As opposed to other metropolises—which Dale respected but ultimately found somewhat repetitive—New Orleans had its own truly unique flair. In addition to the food, there was, of course, the French Quarter, which was known largely for Mardi Gras, but was even more impressive for its architecture and culture. Then there was the music. Jazz weddings and funerals. And, of course, the history. Oh, there was history in New Orleans.

In fact, the entire region was bursting with history. Pensacola—the easternmost city affected by the drugs he and Percy were chasing—was America's first European settlement. Though the city of St. Augustine—farther east in

Florida—was the oldest continuously inhabited European-based settlement in the U.S., Spanish explorer Tristán de Luna founded a settlement in Pensacola six years earlier in 1559.

The area where Dale had found himself marooned for the last couple weeks—the Gulf South—was a historian's dream come true. Plus, there were beautiful beaches. He hadn't had an opportunity to get to one, but he was hoping they might be able to squeeze in half an hour at some point. History, beaches, warm weather—basically, there weren't many better places for Dale to find himself trapped.

But he knew that if he didn't soon come up with some solid evidence that this case was worthy of the BEI's involvement, Percy was indeed going to use the reciprocity clause and take control. Dale couldn't let that happen. Their meeting with the Grizzly had cemented in Dale's mind that this case had a historical connection. He just had to find a way to prove it to Percy. The key lay with the symbols. If he could find a way to prove that the symbols were linked to the drugs and that they were historical in nature, Percy would have to believe him.

Now he just had to figure out how to do that.

He was with Percy at a restaurant, right on the edge of the Mississippi River. The heat had disappeared into the night making the humidity more bearable. They sat at a red picnic table in an outdoor seating area. Lights dangled above, casting the area in a warm glow. There were the sounds of people dining, nighttime insects, and the horns of the riverboats on the water. Sitting beside Percy, to his left, was his seven-year-old daughter, Jeanne. He had his arm behind her. Percy's son Ervin was nowhere to be seen. On his right was his wife Bonita. She was in her mid-forties, like Percy, with gray streaks in her hair and a kind, strong face with a casual beauty.

Percy's family had been in the city for the last week. It proved to be the only chance that year to get the whole family together. They'd been meeting when they could, at night when Percy and Dale tried to give their minds a bit of a reprieve before delving back into the mystery of violent drug deaths and faceless villainy once again.

Now, though, it was time for the family to leave. They were heading back to D.C. the next morning.

Bonita gave Dale a playful scowl. "Three times in as many years you pull my husband away from his family. We have to move to Houston to get some peace and quiet away from you, Dale Conley."

Dale grabbed a miniature cornbread muffin from the bowl in the center of the table and popped it into his mouth. "Don't worry. I won't take it personally."

Percy leaned toward his wife. "So I never think I've seen Dale squirm as much as I did today."

"Oh yeah?" Bonita said with a coy smile. "How's that?"

"I told him we need to bring in Al to help with this case."

Bonita's eyes went wide. "Wait, Al? *The* Al?"

"Mmm-hmm."

"Well, now," Bonita said, staring into Dale with a grin.

"Don't look at me like that. The past is the past." He scanned his surroundings, looking for a way to change the subject. "Where'd Ervin run off to?"

It had been a good fifteen minutes since they'd seen him.

Percy stood up and looked over the area. He pointed. "There he is."

Dale turned around. Ervin was sitting at one of the benches along the sidewalk that lined the river. Dale could see just the back of him, the shape of his massive Afro. He was slouched back, hands in his pockets.

"Mr. Cool," Percy said. "Doesn't have time for his family." He yelled out. "Erv! Come on over and be sociable."

Ervin looked back at them then reluctantly pulled himself up.

Percy shook his head. "And for dessert, how about a little attitude?"

Ervin approached the table. He wore a light yellow butterfly-collar shirt and brown, plaid, flared pants. He was thin in the way only a young man in his late teens could be. He had a mustache, scraggly and sparse. "What's going on, Pops?"

"We're thinking about ordering some banana pudding," Percy said. "House specialty. Want some?"

"Not hungry. Thanks."

Percy breathed in, sighed. He gestured at Dale. "I'm sure Mr. Conley would like to see you before you take off tomorrow."

Ervin slowly turned to Dale, looking down at him from his standing position. "I'm sure he would. Lock anyone up for smoking reefer today? Another government clown like my old man."

"I prefer the term 'government stooge,'" Dale said.

Percy ignored Dale's very clever, ice-breaking gag and stared a hole into Ervin. "Watch your tone, son."

"Don't talk to me like a kid. Are we done here? May I be excused, Daddy?"

Percy waved him off. "Go. Go sulk. Go on."

Ervin turned and left.

Percy watched him leave then looked at Dale. "See what I mean?"

———

Dale and Bonita walked along the sidewalk beside the river, headed back toward the restaurant. A riverboat rolled past, blasting its loud horns. When the horns were through, jazz music came from the top deck, "When the Saints Go Marching In." The song faded away as the boat continued in the opposite direction.

"You bring out a certain quality in Percy that no one else can, Dale."

"What quality is that?"

"Let me put it this way: I've never known my husband to laugh at a fart joke before he met you."

Dale put his hands up, playing innocent. "I take no responsibility. I can't help if my presence brings out his inner dipwad."

She smacked him playfully across the chest. "It always takes him a few days after he's seen you to return to normal. But he likes you, ya know? You've been a good friend to him. And to all of us."

Dale looked ahead of them. Farther up the sidewalk, Percy was sitting on the bench with Ervin, having a serious conversation. Jeanne was a few feet in front of them, scampering, playing by the fence.

"It's easy to do," Dale said. "You're good people."

Bonita smiled at him. "So sweet. I know that at your core you're a big softy."

"A softy? I'm not sure how you heard about that, Bonita, but the doctor assures me it was a one-time thing. Just stress."

"You see? There you go. Hiding with your jokes. You can't fool me, Dale." She smiled at him and took his arm. "Listen, I'm going to ask you for a favor."

"Shoot."

"When Jeanne and I leave tomorrow morning, I want to leave Ervin here with you and Percy."

Dale looked at her.

It had been fine when Percy's whole family was in New Orleans because they only met up like this at night, but if

Ervin were to stay there by himself, that meant that Dale and Percy would have to make a whole lot of accommodations. That could get old really quickly. And besides, it sure didn't seem like Ervin would want to spend time with either Percy or Dale.

"Percy hasn't said anything to me about this."

"He thought I'd have better luck convincing you than him."

Dale chuckled. Percy was clever. Conniving bastard. "Are you sure this is something Ervin wants to do?"

"Oh, he won't want to do it. I'm certain of that. But he needs it. He needs some time with his father. They need to work out this rift between them."

Inwardly, Dale sighed. This would complicate an already complicated situation. But Bonita and the whole Gordon family had been amazing to him, and he was about to say goodbye to them forever. So there was really no choice in the matter. He had to accept it.

"All right, Bonita. Whatever you need."

She smiled, squeezed his arm. "Thank you, Dale."

Dale looked ahead again. Percy and Erv were still having their deep conversation. Percy gestured passionately, earnestly with his hands.

"Doesn't look like Percy is having much luck winning him over."

"Probably not," Bonita said. "He's a headstrong young man. But you're forgetting one thing. He may not listen to his daddy, but he *will* listen to his momma."

CHAPTER ELEVEN

THERE WAS THAT SMELL AGAIN. The smell of piss.

Jesse walked down Bourbon Street in New Orleans. Seven p.m. The sun had only gone down half an hour ago, and while it wasn't terribly crowded, there were still plenty of people out already, going into the shops and bars, some with drinks in their hands. Jesse looked at the people surrounding him and wished them all gone. Far gone. As far away from him as possible.

He stepped into a small store with a sign with large purple letters announcing itself as Voodoo for You. It was a typical New Orleans tourist voodoo shop. Odd trinkets on the walls: candles, voodoo dolls, books. There was a black woman in the back behind a counter. She wore a satiny red ensemble, something flamboyant, made to trick the tourists into thinking that she was a legitimate voodoo queen.

Jesse felt disgusted. Talking to a black person. A black *woman* at that. He reminded himself that this was all in the course of the mission, but he nonetheless fantasized about giving the woman a heaping helping of Dylan's special chemical.

"Welcome to Voodoo for You," the woman said. She spoke with a thick Jamaican accent. "I'm Madame Gertrude. What brings you here today, my dear?"

Jesse slowly walked up to her. He kept a respectable distance. "I was told I could talk to you about the Saint Louis Cemeteries."

"Ooooh, so you've come to see our famous crypts," she said in a sickeningly rich profusion of fake enthusiasm. "Or perhaps you're looking for Marie Laveau." She reached for a brochure among a display to the side of her register. "There are three Saint Louis Cemeteries, and—"

"I'm not looking to tour. I'm looking for symbols."

She stopped flipping through the brochures. Her eyes narrowed. "Symbols?"

"That's right. I was told you were the authority on such matters."

She looked at him for a long moment, and when she spoke again, her Jamaican accent had completely disappeared. "I can't say that I know of any symbols in the cemeteries."

There was something strange about her reaction. Why had she dropped the act so suddenly? And why was there something like fear in her eyes? More importantly, she had no reason to deny that there were symbols in the Saint Louis Cemeteries. Every cemetery was crawling with symbols, especially the ones in New Orleans.

Jesse felt his heart rate quicken. Had he done it again? Was he being careless? He thought of Dylan's ominous words when he had last seen him outside his trailer in Florida.

He composed himself and chose a new course of action. If he had messed up, then he had to get the most out of this encounter.

And then decide how to cut his losses.

"A moon," he said "A symbol of a moon."

She looked at him suspiciously. "I don't know." She paused. "But I heard something else about symbols."

Again, something odd. Something about her tone. Quieter. A bit shaky.

"What have you heard?" he said.

Her eyes lingered on him. "That there's a man. Been going around town asking about symbols. And that this same man is the one behind the bad drugs all those folks are dying from."

Jesse's concern turned to pure panic. But he kept his tone and his composure icy cold. "And have you heard what this man looks like?"

"White ... blond ... brown eyes." There was no mistaking it now. Her voice was shaking. Barely more than a whisper. Fear.

"Interesting. And who would you tell this to?"

"... No one."

Jesse looked around the shop. "Nice shop here. Real nice shop." He turned back to her with a sinister grin then left. He reentered the early-evening revelry on the street. The piss smell.

This was troubling. Extremely troubling.

She recognized him, which meant she'd already heard what Jesse James looked like. Jesse had been careful, but somehow the details of his appearance had already become known around town, even outside of the slums. And now this woman who recognized him had conversed with him at length. Face to face.

And could make a positive identification.

Jesse had already messed things up so bad. He couldn't imagine how Dylan would react if he knew that Jesse had been IDed.

Jesse thought back to the fright he'd tried to give the

woman before he left the shop, his attempt to scare away any future troubles he might get from her. But he wasn't satisfied. It wasn't enough.

He was going to have to take care of this problem.

CHAPTER TWELVE

PERCY RUSHED to keep up with the young uniformed cop who led him and Dale down a dim, dreary high school hallway —green-hued fluorescent lighting, banged-up lockers, cracked flooring. The place was bustling with activity, exploding with noise. They'd had to push through a mob of media to get through the doors, and the corridor was teaming with paramedics, school officials, and police.

Yellow tape crisscrossed one of the classroom doors toward the end of the hall. Nearby stood a disconsolate woman—middle-aged, robust. A cop and a man in a suit stood by, each speaking kindly to her. The woman sobbed loudly.

"Two more deaths," the cop shouted over the chaos. He stepped out of the way of an oncoming firefighter. "Kids. Same symptoms as the others. Bought the shit from another student. They got him here at the school."

Dale turned to Percy, his eyes twinkling with that joy he got when he was stringing together the pieces of a case. "A dealer, Percy! If the kid has bags on him with the same markings as the ones on the bag from the Grizzly, then that means they *are* symbols. And that we have a system for identifying Jesse James' drugs."

"Even if we do find the same markings," Percy said, "you don't know what symbols they are. And we can't have you in the library, Dale. We need you in the field. When are you going to admit that you need Al's help?"

Dale shook his head. "I got a guy who can look into it. I called him up before we left. A real bloodhound. A fellow BEI agent. He'll crack it."

Percy resisted lashing out at Dale. To this point, it had been fun teasing him about his troubled connection with Al, but now Percy was starting to get annoyed. Dale needed to bring Al in as a consultant, but he was avoiding it. And it was starting to piss Percy off.

They pushed past several more people, ducked under the tape, and entered the classroom.

The neat lines of evenly spaced desks were disrupted twice—one desk turned to the side, another lying on the floor. Beside each of the two misplaced desks, on the grimy linoleum, was a body. Teenage boys. About ten feet apart from each other. Older students, maybe seventeen or eighteen years of age. Black.

Percy steeled himself.

Each of the boys' eyes were open. Their limbs were pulled back in awkward positions. Rigor mortis. As he and Dale walked up to the first boy, Percy saw the now standard bloody froth coming from the corner of the boy's mouth. They continued on to the second boy. The same grimace. The same bloody froth.

Percy glanced at Dale. His expression had changed dramatically from the excited grin he'd been wearing in the hallway about the prospect of finding more symbols. Now his face was grim as he looked down at the boys, his lips pulled tight into a thin line.

"Goddamn nightmare," the cop said. He took his cap off and wiped his brow. "That's the local media outside, but within a couple hours every national outlet will be here. They're already calling. Everyone listens when it's kids who are dying."

"What happened?" Dale said, looking down at the nearest body.

The cop stepped closer. "After-school program. The kids came back from a twenty-minute break. Class starts back up. The teacher said it wasn't ten minutes after they all got back into the room that one of them started shaking, fell out of his seat." He looked at his notes. "Darrell Coleman. Then it happened with the other kid, Lewis Ball. Kids started screaming, running out. The kid who sold it to them was one of their best friends. It's a damn tragedy."

"Where's the friend?" Percy said.

"They got him in a classroom."

———

Percy and Dale stepped into the room and shut the door behind them. It was a science lab—desks in the center and lab stations lining the walls. In one of the desks was a teenage boy. Thin, wearing a blue-and-white ringer T-shirt and green pants. He was slouched in his seat, his head hung down to his chest, and his hands were shoved into his pockets. But there was one thing about the boy that took Percy completely by surprise.

He was black.

Immediately Percy's mind struggled with a paradox—if this kid was black and he was one of the people selling the rotten drugs, that completely shot his and Dale's theory that the drug deaths were race-related poisonings.

Percy looked at Dale. His expression was stunned.

Standing behind the boy was Detective Snyder, one of the principal NOPD narcotics officers on the task force. Snyder was in his late thirties with feathery, sandy-colored hair and deep-set eyes. He always looked a little bit stressed. He walked over to them.

"Agent Conley. Agent Gordon."

"Snyder."

"He's not talking. I didn't press him too much. I figured I'd leave that to the feds," he said with a bit of a mischievous look. "It's your task force, after all." Snyder was the type of local cop who liked to give feds grief. But it was mostly good-natured. Mostly.

"Name?" Percy said, flicking his eyes toward the kid.

"Byron Mitchell."

"Find anything on him?" Dale said.

Snyder nodded an affirmative and stepped away.

Percy and Dale stepped over to the boy, turned a couple desks around to face him, and sat down.

"Bryon," Percy said, "may we have a word?"

He shrugged and didn't look up. They saw just the top of his head.

"Tell us about the drugs," Dale said.

Byron didn't answer, still didn't look up. His hands remained shoved in his pockets, shoulders slumped forward. His headstrong demeanor reminded Percy of Ervin.

"Whatever you're a part of, Byron," Dale said, "whatever all these poisonings are about, the more you cooperate with us, the better things are going to turn out for you."

The boy finally looked at them. His expression was impudent, but his proud eyes were full of tears. "Man, I *didn't know*." His eyes darted around the classroom. His breaths were short and choppy. "I didn't think this was the same pot that's been killing people. It's been bums so far who died. Not high school kids."

"You got the drugs from someone else?" Dale said.

Byron nodded. "A few days ago I met this guy through my dealer. Supposed to have some real good stuff. He gave me a bag with a little in it. A sample, you know? Good shit. Yesterday I go to this guy to get some more. He says he wants me to start selling at the school. Said he'd pay me. The money was good, man. So..." He stopped and looked away. A tear fell down his cheek. He wiped it away violently, embarrassed. "So I sold some to Darrel and Louie tonight. They lit up, and ... right away they both said they didn't feel right."

"Did you smoke any?" Percy said.

"I smoked the first bag the guy gave me. But I didn't smoke any tonight. I was about to. But when they said they felt weird, I thought about all those people dying. And I realized I'd sold them some of the killer stuff. I'm telling you, I didn't know." He wiped away more tears.

"The man who gave you the drugs," Dale said. "What did he look like?"

"White dude. Blond, parted hair."

Percy and Dale exchanged another glance.

"Did he give you a name?"

"No."

There was a noise from the back. Snyder came in. He had two evidence bags in his hand. Percy and Dale stood up. Snyder stepped over and handed the bags to Dale. Inside of each was a smaller clear plastic bag of the same size and shape as the bag they'd gotten from the Grizzly. One was filled with pot; the other was empty, just residue.

Percy put his hand on Byron's shoulder. "Good luck, Byron."

He was being genuine. No matter what happened, no matter how the law sorted things out, Byron now had to go through life knowing he'd accidentally killed two of his best friends.

"And don't worry," Percy added. "We're going to catch this guy."

Back in the hallway, Dale stopped beneath one of the ceiling lights and held up the bags. He grinned and handed them to Percy. "What did I tell you, Percy? They're the same markings."

Dale was right. There were the markings again, one set in the upper and lower corners of each bag. They were of the same style as those on the bag from the Grizzly—small dots and lines, scored into the plastic, clearly written by hand. None of the four sets of markings matched.

The empty bag had dots and lines both on the top ...

... and bottom.

The other bag had a corner shape, possibly an L, along with a dot on the top ...

... and a slash and a backwards 6 on the bottom.

Percy nodded reluctantly. Sometimes he hated when Dale was right. His ego was large enough as it was. Still, he'd cracked the case. They had a method of identifying Jesse James' drugs.

So Percy couldn't help but smile.

Dale pumped a fist. "I knew it. Symbols. This is our confirmation, Percy. We let people know that any pot in bags with these markings are from Jesse James. And now," he said, pointing toward the front of the school, "we have a national media at our disposal to get that message out. I hope you're ready to hold a press conference, handsome."

CHAPTER THIRTEEN

DYLAN LOOKED at the beautiful scene before him—a bright moon hanging in a partially clouded sky, shining down on the gentle waves of Pensacola Bay—interrupted by a decrepit stretch of green, rusted metal. The hood of his piece of shit car.

It was a 1960 Chevy Corvair. He'd gotten it not long after he moved to Florida, twelve years earlier, from Indiana. It became his a couple months after he met Luanne. It had been sitting in her uncle's barn, not running. The rebuilt transmission had gotten it working again, and it had been clinging to life ever since. The interior—with its cracked seats and stained dashboard—still smelled musty. The light green paint was riddled with decay. The driver's side door was almost entirely rust-covered, and, unlike the rest of the car, this replacement door had been red at one point.

He hated the car. And he hated that he hadn't been able to get anything better in over a decade. Coming to Florida had been an escape after he lost his job at Eli Lilly pharmaceutical company in Indianapolis. They'd screwed him, not giving him even a chance to repair the damage he had done, leaving him overqualified for anything but a shit job and underqualified for any new career of substance. A master's degree and nothing to do with it. His family in Indiana was worthless white trash, and he had nothing tying him to the area. But he had a buddy in Pensacola, Florida. What better place to restart. Beaches. Winters free of snow and ice. His buddy had been a family friend, so when Dylan got to Pensacola, he found himself falling into the same circles that he had tried so hard to escape in Indiana by educating himself, pursuing a career, wearing the right clothes, acting the right way. He was back to slum bars. He was back to wasted days sitting in lawn chairs, staring at a backyard, discussing worthless nonsense with worthless people and getting nowhere. And the people he found himself with in Florida were even worse than those in Indiana. When he was in Pensacola, the people were fine. But the people he was hanging around weren't in the city. They were north of that. In the trees. Good ol' boys. Dylan hated Southerners. He hated their accent. He hated their demeanor. And he hated that he found himself in a de facto situation of being required to spend time with them. He'd been at the pinnacle with his job and his education. Living in a metropolis. With a big degree and a big title and big responsibilities.

And yet here he was, somehow married to a backwoods idiot who shit out two of his kids, one of them a goddamn weakling.

He looked at Luanne now, sitting beside him in the passenger seat. She'd gained a few pounds and several wrinkles, but she was still decent looking. That was, of course, why he'd dated her in the first place. She met his sexual needs, doing everything he wanted, even the weirder shit. She didn't do it well, but she did it. All around, she was fairly helpful, and she was a decent cook. But she was meek and simple. And a Southerner.

In the back seat were his sons. Tyler was five years old, a little roughneck with a mischievous smile. Dylan's little partner. Tyler had grown the back of his hair into a rattail, which Dylan didn't like. It was a redneck hairstyle. But he'd allowed it. If Dylan was going to get out of this mess, he had to fit in with the Southerners. So letting his youngest grow out a rattail was a small sacrifice.

Hell, he already lived in a trailer.

Next to Tyler was eleven-year-old Caleb. His little sissy boy. Caleb liked to draw. He liked to watch cartoons instead of spending time outside. He had school friends who were girls but no girlfriends. He spent too much time with Luanne. And Luanne babied the shit out of him.

They were parked outside Pensacola Municipal Auditorium, a grand entertainment venue that brought world-famous acts to the city. Elvis had visited in the '50s. It was built at the end of Palafox Street, right into the bay, surrounded on all sides by water. A drive wrapped all the way around the building, and it had numerous parking spots and a wide walkway with a fence that went right up the water's edge, making it a popular spot for scenic views of the water. But Dylan's purpose that night was altogether different. He kept watching the corner of the walkway where he was to meet the investors. People walked by—couples holding hands, families walking their dogs—but the other men had still not shown.

He'd been there in the car with his family for twenty minutes. The investors hadn't given him a precise time. Dylan could tell that Luanne was getting antsy. She had that look on her face, the one she wore before she was about to whine. She was always bitching about something.

"Can't we go in some of the stores? It's muggy. And the boys don't get to come here often."

"I said to stay put. It's bad enough I gotta look like an imbecile bringing my family with me to something professional like this." He looked through the windshield again to the corner where he was to meet the investors. They still hadn't arrived.

"These boys gotta see the doctor," Luanne said with a little laugh. "It's only once a year."

Dylan didn't appreciate her tone—laughing at him—and he let her know by the look he gave her. The smartass grin on her face disappeared. She looked at her hands.

"You gonna buy us a second car, Luanne?" he said. "If we had one, none of this would be a problem. Unless you got some inheritance I've not heard about from that lovely family of yours, we're stuck in this predicament. So stay in the car for a few minutes, and shut your goddamn mouth."

"I'm sorry, baby. We ain't going anywhere. I promise." She put a hand on his knee.

Through the windshield, Dylan saw four men in suits approach the corner. He opened the door. "Stop saying 'ain't.' You sound like a hillbilly."

He left the car, shutting the door harder than he had to.

———

Dylan walked to the corner. The men watched him as he approached, standing beyond by the decorative fencing that traced the water's edge. Four of them. All in their sixties and seventies. All native Southerners. All loaded with money. Three of them wore blank expressions. One of them—the fattest of them, the one with all-white hair—had a smug, condescending smile.

Dylan knew only one of their names. Mick Henderson. The one on the far right. He was in his early sixties, probably the youngest of the four. He was refined—in a back-slapping, hand-shaking kind of way. The sort of man who makes deals. Round cheeks. An extra chin. A hint of twinkle to his blue eyes. Dylan had met with him a couple times, and as he stepped closer to the group, the two of them exchanged a look for the briefest of moments. The other three had no idea of their connection and hadn't expected anything when Henderson agreed to be the contact person between the investors and Dylan.

"We're losing our faith in you, Mercer," the fat one said.

"I know, and—"

"Word has it that the deaths are starting to get traced back to your organization," said the small, frail-looking one with liver-spotted skin. "That your man Jesse James is gaining a reputation on the streets."

"I've had a chat with Richter. He knows the price of his current actions."

The fat one spoke again. "Nine months ago we get word of an out-of-work chemist from Indiana with a plan for those of means and a concern about the proliferation of the Negro population over the last one hundred years. You convinced us that you could control your group of simpletons who would join your age-old secret organization. Give them structure. A sense of purpose. Rankings. Uniforms. That you could then use them to distribute your deadly drugs. What you didn't tell us was that you'd be so sloppy. That you'd let the rednecks you've contracted give us away."

"We're so close now to the final stage. You have my word that I'll take care of this. I can reign in Jesse Richter."

"And what is this I hear of symbols?" said the one with the beard. He had a raspy voice. "That you have Richter out looking for markings on trees and tombstones?"

"All part of the lore. The group was steeped in symbols

and mythology. The more the hillbillies believe, the easier it is to control them," Dylan said.

"You'd better hope you can control them, Mercer," the fat one said. "For your own sake. We aren't men you want to cross."

CHAPTER FOURTEEN

Luanne Mercer felt ashamed.

In her hand was the piece of paper she'd seen lodged in the gap beside the driver's seat. Something about it had caught her eye. A marking. In blue ink. It wasn't writing. It was a drawing, some sort of doodle. She wanted to know what it was. It wasn't right, her taking this paper and examining it, but she had never known her husband to draw anything in the entire time they had been together. In fact, the thought of him doing anything artistic was laughable. So why was there a drawing on this paper?

Her eyes flicked up to the windshield again. She saw that her husband was still having his meeting with the four suited men. They stood by the fence along the walkway that overlooked the bay. Their conversation looked serious.

She was being sneaky. She didn't know what had come into her, choosing to grab this piece of paper that belonged to Dylan. And the more times she looked up to check if he was coming, the more it solidified her feeling that she was doing something wrong.

But she was going to do it anyway. Bizarre curiosity had

grabbed her in a stranglehold, and Dylan hadn't been treating her well lately. It was okay for her to look. Just a little.

She unfolded the paper. On it, in Dylan's handwriting, was a list of locations. Beside the names were strange little drawings.

All the places on the list were in the region. They could very well be related to his work, but she couldn't imagine why he'd have business in Marianna, of all places. It was a small city. Real small. And it was two hours to the east. Dylan had put a question mark next to its name on the list. New Orleans—which made much better sense as a business location—was three hours to the west. Naval Live Oaks was much closer, about fifteen minutes from Pensacola and half an hour from where Dylan and Luanne lived outside Cantonment. But unlike the other places, it wasn't even a city. It was a park, part of the National Seashore. Each of the locations except New Orleans had one of the small drawings beside it. There was something slightly creepy about them. Almost sinister. They gave Luanne a disconcerted feeling.

She looked up again. Dylan's meeting was dispersing, and

he was heading toward the car. She folded the paper in half again and put it back against the driver's seat.

Luanne got a better look at the men as they crossed beneath the glow of the lamps that were spaced around the walkway. She recognized one of the faces. Mick Henderson. A local developer. One of the wealthiest men in Pensacola.

She leaned forward. She had to be mistaken. Surely that wasn't *Mick Henderson*. Why in the world would he have business with her husband, a man with a work-from-home position shipping pharmaceuticals?

But it was him. Clear as day. Mick Henderson.

"What is it, Momma?" Caleb said from the backseat.

Luanne sat back in her seat. "Nothing, honey."

There was something going on with her husband lately. She could tell it in the way he'd been acting. And now there was the list of cities with the weird drawings—and the fact that he was meeting with someone as powerful as Mick Henderson.

Something very strange was happening.

CHAPTER FIFTEEN

IT WAS A TOWERING CEILING, reaching up to a rounded point, half an oval, like the outline of the narrow end of an egg. It stretched down far on either side of Dale, a gigantic, geometric, chic hallway. The massive wall at the end was a latticework of weaving, angular designs which would have let in sunlight during the day but now showed black sky beyond. There was an enormous bank of lights suspended from the ceiling. Stores lined either side, and rows of cushioned seats zigzagged through the center.

Dale and Percy sat in these seats, and they looked out into the swarming mass of people crisscrossing the floors of New Orleans International Airport, watching for Dale's contact. Sitting beside Percy, with a buffer space of a full five feet, was Ervin. He too was staring into the crowd. But he was glassy-eyed. Bored. Angry. His legs were crossed in front of him, and his hands were clasped behind his head, fingers buried in his Afro.

Dale leaned around Percy. "You like coming to airports, Erv?"

He didn't respond.

"Gives you a chance to do some people watching," Dale said. "You gotta wonder where all these people are going."

"Yeah," Ervin muttered without looking at him. "Fun stuff."

Dale gave him a thumbs-up. "Okie dokie."

He looked at Percy, who sighed.

Dale returned to searching the crowd for his contact. And there he was. Halfway down the hallway. The man was hard to miss, even among the varied, international mix of people surrounding them.

Dark red pants. Dark red shirt. Dark red, plastic-framed eyeglasses. An elegant yet awkward stride. Pompous but weird. His name was Marty Rhodes. He saw Dale and changed his trajectory, headed toward him.

Dale and Percy stood up, and Marty stopped in front of Dale. "Where are my peaches?"

His voice was lofty and tinged with melodrama, as though he was always taking life about ten percent too seriously.

"I'm afraid I don't have them, Marty."

"You said you'd bring me peaches, Dale. Last month. When you had that case in Atlanta. I asked you to bring me some fresh peaches, and, Dale, you said that you would. Do you remember?"

"I remember."

"You forgot, Dale. And I didn't get my peaches. I still don't have my peaches."

"There's a fruit stand right down the street from the BEI office back in D.C. You can pick some up when you get back."

"Oh, it's not the same, and you know it's not the same." Marty paused and frowned. "I don't like being forgotten." His attention turned to Percy for the first time. "Who's the stiff?"

"The stiff is Percy Gordon with the DEA," Dale said and put his hand on Percy's shoulder, guided him over. "Percy, meet Special Agent Marty Rhodes, one of my six associates at the BEI. One of the world's foremost minds in the field of art theory and history. You can call him Arty Marty."

"You're the only one who calls me that, Dale. And you know I hate it." Marty reached his hand out to Percy, half-heartedly. "Charmed, I'm sure."

Percy, clearly objecting to being called a stiff, looked Marty up and down. "You like red, do you?"

Marty eyeballed him. He turned away before answering. "Maroon."

"Who you callin' a maroon?"

"The color," Dale answered for him. "Marty is in his maroon period."

Percy glanced over Marty's clothes again, chewing his gum slowly. "Maroon. Not red?"

Marty didn't reply, continued staring in the opposite direction.

"Marty ran through all the primary, secondary, and tertiary colors a long time ago," Dale said. "He's had to get more specific. Maroon, puce, taupe." He looked at Marty. "This period's been going on for, what, a few weeks now?"

Marty rolled his eyes. "Almost three months. Again, thanks for paying attention, Dale. You're a true friend and associate. My periods are lengthy."

Dale snickered. "Must be why you're so salty."

Percy broke a smile. "I bet an all-maroon outfit really comes in handy out in the field."

Marty still ignored Percy.

"Actually," Dale said, "Marty's a master of disguise in the field. I go to him whenever I need undercover makeup. By the way, you need to work on that mustache adhesive."

"You need to learn to apply it better," Marty said.

"Touché." Dale turned to Percy. "Marty and I end up combining our talents a lot. Art and history are intrinsically connected."

"And you turn me into your research assistant whenever I'm not working a case," Marty said, his voice diving even deeper into self-pity.

"Did you get me the Civil War documents I need?"

"Yes, Dale. The materials were on the jet with me. They're already being chartered to the office you're using."

"Thank ya kindly."

Good ol' Arty Marty. Dale could always count on him.

"And I brought someone with me," Marty said. A wicked smile crept from the corners of his mouth.

"Who?" Dale said.

But he already knew who Marty had brought. He knew why Marty was giving him a retributive grin.

A deep voice came from the crowd.

"Conley!"

Dale, Marty, and Percy all looked. And saw him coming toward them.

Special Agent in Charge Walter Taft. Dale's boss. He was about forty feet away, pushing his way through the crowd. He was in his fifties—paunchy and oily with gray-red hair and a face that was permanently fixed with an expression of frustrated exasperation. He wore a short-sleeve dress shirt with thin vertical stripes, unbuttoned at the top, and a wide, brown tie. His bald forehead shined brightly under the big lights hanging from the ceiling. His eyes were fixed on Dale. His teeth were bared.

"He insisted on coming with," Marty said.

Taft pushed past the last people blocking him and stepped right up to Dale. "Conley, what in the name of all that's holy are you doing down here?"

Dale smiled. "Sir, you seem perturbed."

"Two weeks," Taft spat, holding up a pair of fingers. "Two weeks you've been down here, and the only updates I get from you are that you're making 'further developments.' And, conveniently, those phone calls only come in when I'm out of the office. I need some substance, pretty boy. I need you to tell me exactly why the U.S. taxpayers are continuing to fund your little New Orleans trip."

"Well, sir, I've just recently made some ... further developments."

Taft growled. "Conley, I ought to—"

Percy interjected. "Sir, just tonight Agent Conley made a major break in the case. He discovered a system of symbols on the drug bags."

"That's right," Dale said with another big smile, putting a reassuring hand on Taft's shoulder. Taft glared at the hand. Dale removed it. "Percy here is going to hold a press conference later tonight. The public will know that any drugs with these symbols came from Jesse James. Now we need to figure out the meaning of the symbols. Which is why I brought Marty onboard."

"You didn't even get me my peaches," Marty said. "Why should I help you?"

"Because you're required to."

Marty grumbled.

———

Dale, Marty, and Taft were at one of the long rows of cushioned seats in the middle of the corridor. Ervin sat by himself at the row of seats across the hall, several feet away, ignoring them. Percy had left to call into the station. The bags of drugs sat on Marty's maroon-clad lap. He was bent over, scrutinizing the symbols, squinting through his oversized glasses. He'd been like this for a several long minutes, in an almost trance-like state. The other three were quiet, giving the genius a few moments to process his inspection. Taft's arms were crossed, and he picked at his thumbnail. The eccentricities of the agents under his charge annoyed the living hell out of him.

Finally, Marty sat up.

"Like I told you on the phone," he said to Dale. "I have no clue what these symbols could be. They're like nothing I've ever seen."

"But I *know* I've seen them before," Dale said. "Come on, Marty. Think."

Marty shrugged. "I haven't the foggiest idea. Frankly, I can't believe you flew me all the way here for this. It's not my expertise. Or yours. This isn't art or history. This is symbology." He thought for a moment. Then his eyes lit up. "I know who you ought to bring in to help."

Oh no ...

"That treasure hunter!" Marty said, quite pleased with the brilliance of his idea. "The one from that heroin assignment you had. Unless you totally burnt that bridge."

Al. Al. Everyone wanted him to bring in Al. Fine. Dale was a stubborn man, but he knew when he needed to admit defeat.

He turned to Taft. "Sir, I need a consultant. I need to bring in—"

"Al Blair?" Taft said. "It's already done. Al got down here a couple hours ago. Here's the phone number for the hotel." He reached into his pocket, took out a scrap of paper.

Dale stared at him, confused. "But how..." He trailed off. And then his mind put the pieces together. "Percy."

Taft nodded.

Percy. That son of a bitch. Dale smiled though. Percy was a clever rascal, but he usually made the right call. Even when Dale disagreed.

And there he was.

Percy sprinted up to them. Out of breath. "We gotta go. Now."

"What's going on?" Dale said.

"The Grizzly came through for us. Phoned in a tip. There's a deal going down. Got an address. But we only have twenty minutes."

Dale's eyes lit up, and he jumped out of his seat.

Percy turned to Ervin. "Stay here. We'll come back for you."

"Whatever, man."

Dale smacked Taft on the shoulder. "Sorry, sir. Duty calls."

Dale and Percy dashed off down the hall.

CHAPTER SIXTEEN

THE MIDDLE of the night on Bourbon Street. Jesse had returned.

There was the typical drunken madness. Crowds walking down the streets, stumbling. Laughter, shouting. Sloshing drinks. Slovenly acts of passion.

Jesse stood to the side, leaning against a pole supporting one of the famous second-floor balconies. He was the only static person in a swarming mass of hysteria. He glanced at the pole in front of him where, several feet up, there was a wreath of metal spikes. During one of his trips to Bourbon Street, he'd passed by a tour group, and he overheard the guide explain that those pointed pieces of metal were "Romeo Spikes" and in the past had been a father's means of keeping amorous admirers of their daughters from climbing the poles to the second floor. Even the history of New Orleans, even its architecture, was steeped in debauchery.

He'd been leaning against the pole for half an hour, staring at the entrance of Voodoo for You, a block and a half away. A brochure he grabbed earlier noted that Madame Gertrude held her readings from 5 to 9 p.m. He checked his watch. 9:17.

Madam Gertrude exited the store. She stopped at the door, looked back inside, and said a few words to someone within. She turned to leave.

Her gaze shifted to her right for a moment—and she saw Jesse. Their eyes met. She quickly headed in the opposite direction.

Jesse sprung into action. He couldn't spare a moment. She'd spotted him. This complicated matters a lot. But he'd be fine if he kept his cool. He followed her, pushing his way through the crowds.

She was about a block ahead of him. She used her hands to clear people out of her way. Her vibrant outfit made her stand out even among the other flamboyantly-dressed people. She looked behind her, made eye contact with him again. She was afraid.

A wave of people stumbled in front of Jesse, some sort of group, about half a dozen men wearing matching pink T-shirts. Jesse shoved one of them, knocking him over.

"Get the hell out of my way."

He moved past the group. From behind, there were shouts of anger. He ignored them, looked forward. Madam Gertrude was nowhere to be seen.

He felt a wave of panic. But he continued to push forward.

He went to the next cross street, Toulouse Street, peered down it. More crowds. More drunks. Then he spotted her ... talking to a cop.

Madame Gertrude and the cop both looked his direction. And spotted him. The cop started toward him.

Change of plans.

Jesse took off again, continuing down Bourbon Street. He slipped through the crowd. A doorway to his left, the entrance to a bar. He took a turn around a large woman wearing a mask and a dress made of faux peacock feathers and stepped into the building.

Loud music. Laughter. The place was thick with people, and Jesse grimaced as he squeezed between them, feeling them pressed against him. Sweat. Shoulders. Beer breath. The bar was to his right, and he spied a bit of space. He shouldered his way in and put an elbow on the bar. He halfheartedly waved at one of the bartenders. She acknowledged him, continued with her current drink order.

While he waited, he watched the bar's open doorway. The cop walked past.

Jesse exhaled.

He'd avoided immediate disaster, but he knew that things were going to escalate soon. Dylan *would* find out about this. Jesse thought again about the ominous warnings he'd been given in Florida. This business with Madame Gertrude would prove disastrous for him—unless he took measures to protect his reputation. He was going to have to do something preemptive. Something bold and decisive. A new course of action, something to show Dylan how valuable a leader Jesse really was to the organization.

Jesse was going to do something drastic. He was going to shake things up. And he was going to do it tonight.

CHAPTER SEVENTEEN

DALE'S CHEST HEAVED, and his feet ached as they pounded the pavement. Another group of people on the sidewalk in front of him—bathed in the orange glow of a streetlight— watched him as he flew by. They'd already cleared the way for the man Dale was chasing.

The guy was in his twenties, about six-foot tall, and white. He wore jeans and a paisley shirt. His hair color was brown, which meant he wasn't Jesse James. He was fifty feet ahead of Dale and getting away. Dale was a fast runner, but this guy was in excellent shape and had the threat of the law biting at his heels. Fear was a strong motivator.

Dale looked back. Percy was behind him by maybe another fifty feet or so. He was nowhere near Dale's fitness level. His face was tortured, sweating profusely. Poor guy. They'd been chasing the dealer for almost two miles.

Farther behind Percy was another person running after them, a coarse-looking woman in a drab dress. The dealer's old lady. When they'd approached the dealer and his mark, right as the drugs were about to change hands, she'd been with him. The dealer bolted, leaving her behind. Ever the faithful companion, she took chase after Dale and Percy. Screaming. She hadn't stopped.

"Leave him alone! He ain't done nothing! You leave him alone!"

She was the slowest among them, the caboose pulling up the rear of their train of people sprinting down the street in a shithole part of New Orleans. Dale pictured what this whole scene must look like to the bystanders, and it looked absurd. The Benny Hill theme—"Yakety Sax"—played in his head.

"Leave him alone!"

Ahead of Dale, the dealer pulled to the side as he ran, going toward a trash can. He threw something at the can, missing. The item fluttered to the ground. A plastic bag.

Dale yelled out behind him. "Grab it, Percy!"

He couldn't risk losing the guy. Percy was farther back and the slower runner. He could pick it up.

Moments later, after Dale had sprinted past the trash can, he looked back and saw Percy grab the bag before continuing the chase. Dale noticed that the screaming had ceased. The woman had given up. She was much farther back, stopped, bent over with her hands on her knees.

But now there was barking. Behind Percy, a dog had picked up where the woman left off. Evidentially they'd excited it as they ran past wherever it called home. It was a vicious thing. Squat, muscly. A good candidate for a junkyard dog. And it was gaining on Percy. Fast.

Shit.

Percy had seen it too. His eyes were wide. Clearly the threat of the dog had awoken some reserves deep in Percy's middle-aged legs because he was starting to catch up with Dale. Fear was indeed a strong motivator.

Ahead, the dealer took a left into an alley. Another group of people screamed as Dale ran past them, tracing the other man's path. There was a tall fence—about ten feet—at the far end of the alley. To the right side was a phone booth. The dealer made it to the fence and sprung upon it with a frantic leap. He scrambled up the chainlink.

This would give Dale a chance.

He ran up to the fence as the man was almost to the top. He grabbed the man's left shoe with one hand, the fence with the other. Pulled. The dealer smashed his free foot into Dale's face. A sharp pulse of pain. The man yanked himself free.

Barking. Harsh barking from behind.

Percy and the dog had entered the alley. Drool flung from the dog's snapping teeth. Percy's eyes were saucers of fright. His legs kicked furiously.

Dale looked up. The dealer cleared the top of the fence.

Then there was a flurry of action, so fast that Dale wasn't sure how it had happened. He turned. There was Percy. Those huge eyes, scared shitless. His mouth was open, screaming unintelligible words. The dog's mouth, too, was open. Rows of sharp teeth. Piercing barks. To the side was the phone booth. Dale was moving. The dog was close. The door of the phone booth. Squeezed inside. Something next to him. Warmth, human touch. Screeching as the door shut. His cheek slammed against the glass. Neck twisted uncomfortably. Percy pressed up against him. Barking, inches away. Incessant. Scratching of claws on glass.

Dale's senses returned as the chaos congealed. A realization. He was squeezed into a phone booth with Percy. And he was trapped. The exit was guarded by a ravenous hellhound. Cerberus himself.

The phone booth shook. Puffs of steam appeared on the glass from the pouncing demon's hungry breath.

Dale couldn't assess the situation fully, as his face was cemented against the back side of the phone booth. His view was of the dark brick of the alley wall, a few inches away. He could feel that his legs were contorted, one of Percy's legs lodged between them. His right arm was pulled behind his back, held in place by Percy's chest. The side of the telephone dug into his shoulder. More barking, scratching from outside.

"What the hell do we do now?" Percy said.

Dale summoned his quick-thinking again. "There's no better place to get trapped than a phone booth. I have a dime. We can call the station."

"The *station?*" Percy said. "And have other cops come and rescue us. No. You and I are operating a task force out of this city. I want to maintain some level of respect. You know who was always good with animals?"

Dale had managed to remain calm after being twisted into a pretzel with another man within a coffin-sized structure guarded by a mad beast, but Percy's broaching of this topic again made him lose his patience. "Oh god. We're in a situation like this, and you're bringing up Al *again?*"

"Taft gave you the hotel's phone number."

"Absolutely not. We're calling the station. I'm still the lead agent. You're gonna have to get the dime. My arm's stuck. Front right pocket."

Dale felt Percy's hand slide from the middle of his back toward his 501s.

"Fresh," Dale said.

The hand plunged into Dale's pocket. Both men grunted with discomfort. The hand went lower.

"Hey!" Dale said as the hand reached the bottom of his pocket. "You didn't even buy me dinner."

Then a noise came from outside. The *blip* of a police siren. It came from the end of the alley.

Percy's hand quickly retracted. "Saved by the bell," he said.

The dog continued to bark savagely as Dale stared at the bricks and listened intently to what was happening outside.

Footsteps approached. Slowly, cautiously. Then stopped. Several feet away.

The barking got quieter. And quieter. And ceased. It was replaced by a low growl, almost a whimper. There was the sound of the dog's feet padding away. It whined for a few moments longer and stopped. Silence. Then a voice came. A voice very familiar to Dale.

Three words. Bemused but incredibly annoyed, as though the situation in which Dale had found himself was somehow so ludicrous that it offended the sensibilities of the voice's owner.

"Oh. My. God."

It was a female voice. Dale's ex-girlfriend.

It was Al.

CHAPTER EIGHTEEN

A DIFFERENT VOICE, a man's voice, called out from the alley. "The coast is clear, Agents."

There was movement against Dale's back as Percy opened the phone booth door then stumbled outside. Dale felt a wave of relief as the pressure of Percy's body left him. He stepped out of the phone booth and grabbed his neck. Then he looked to his left.

In the dim light of the alley, he saw her.

Allison Blair.

Everyone called her Allie. Except for Dale. He'd called her Al.

She was knelt over. The dog was in front of her, and she rubbed its ears. It licked at her hands, tail wagging. Behind her were two cops. Young guys. One white, one black. They were snickering at Dale and Percy, trying to hide it.

When you haven't seen someone in a long time, there's always a moment of quiet reconciling, a split second when your brain rectifies the memories with the irrefutable new truth of the person standing before you. Dale had never experienced this sensation with a former girlfriend before because, though Dale had done more than his fair share of dating, Al was the only girlfriend he'd ever had.

There was just a split second between the moment he exited the phone booth to when she turned her attention to him. He studied her in this frozen bit of time while her eyes were still cast down at the dog. Her hair was shorter. Shoulder-length. Curly, dark red, and untamable. It had been midway down her back when they were together, and the new, shorter length made it even wilder, pushing away from her head with an unrestrained volume must have been difficult for her to maintain but nonetheless looked great on her, framing her round face. She wore a light blue T-shirt with a deep V-neck and a pair of bellbottom blue jeans. Her curves. Freckles, on her arms, her face, just visible in the darkness. The tops of her eyelids, as she looked down at the dog. Long eyelashes that blinked once as she looked up and saw him.

Their eyes met.

She stood up.

"Al?"

"Dale, what do you think you're doing?" she said. There was the voice. Sweet but bordering on shrill. Familiar. "Are you a dog trainer now, Dale? Locked in a phone booth. My god, Dale."

Three times. Three times in four sentences she'd used his name. This was the annoyed Al. She always punctuated her sentences with his name when she was annoyed with him. And his antics annoyed her more than anything else because—

Dale stopped his train of thought right where it was.

"Why are you here?" he said, his eyes turning toward the cops as the words came out.

One of the cops took his meaning. "She was already at the station," he said. "Trying to find you. Someone called in your foot chase. When she heard your name and the phone booth situation, she insisted on coming. *Insisted*." The cop gave him a look.

Dale understood what the cop was getting at. When Al insisted on something, she was going to get it.

He looked at her. "Why are you here?" he said again.

"Well, that's a fine how-do-you-do after all this time. You don't need to be a mean green bean."

Her phrases. Little cutesy expressions like that. *Mean green bean*. He'd forgotten about those.

Dale just looked at her.

"It's nice to see you," she said.

More memories rushed back into Dale's brain. Less pleasant things. "I believe the last thing you told me was you never wanted to see me again."

Al crossed her arms. "No, you asked me if I ever wanted to see you again. I said no."

"It means the same, Al."

"Don't call me that. My name's Allie. You're the only person who's ever called me Al. Well, you and your little buddy here." She looked at Percy.

"Hi Al," Percy said.

She scowled.

"All right, all right," Dale said. "'Allie' it is."

She turned back to Dale. They stared at each other, both of them making assessments, calculating their thoughts and words. Dale glanced at the cops. They were incredibly uncomfortable.

Allie took a deep breath. "You look good."

"I do, don't I?" Dale said and pumped up a little bit. He winked at Percy. "You know what they say. Men age like wine; women age like milk."

"Oh, a little quip. Surprise, surprise. That took you all of a minute," Allie said and looked at her wrist. She wasn't wearing a watch. She took a step toward him, put her hands on her hips. "And a mean quip too. Who says something like that? You're such a prick, Dale."

"Come on, Al. I was—"

"Allie."

"Allie, I was joking. Don't be so sensitive. You look good too."

Allie rolled her eyes. "Thanks."

One of the cops cleared his throat. He pointed at his wrist, which actually *was* bearing a watch. "Sir?"

"Yeah, Dale," Allie said with a mischievous, slightly wicked grin. "I don't see any bad guys. You got anything to show for getting trapped in a phone booth by this little creature here?"

The dog had followed her and sat by her feet. Her fingers rested atop its head, carelessly playing with its fur. The dog growled at Dale when he looked down at it.

Dale remembered the bag that he and Percy retrieved. A jolt of excitement rushed over him.

"As a matter of fact, I do," he said and looked at Percy.

Percy reached into his suit jacket and handed him the bag then said, "I gotta run. Press conference in an hour, and I need to pick Erv up first."

"Right," Dale said. He'd forgotten about that. The giddiness of historical intrigue always gave Dale touches of amnesia. "Yeah, go. I'll see you back at the office."

Percy nodded at Allie and walked off.

Dale stepped a few feet away, stood beneath a lamp. He held the bag above his head, to the light.

More symbols, at the top ...

... and bottom of the bag.

Dale smiled. Another jolt of excitement rushed through his system. "Allie, check this out."

He almost called her Al again. Old habits die hard.

Allie frowned and approached him, but when she saw the markings on the bag, her face lit up. The treasure hunter in her took over. She snatched it from him. Her eyes went wide with awe.

"They're symbols, aren't they?" Dale said.

Allie nodded quickly, enthusiastically. "They most certainly are."

"Told you so, Percy!" Dale yelled out to his partner, who was at the end of the alley, rounding the corner. Percy shook his head.

Dale stuck out his tongue.

"So what kind of symbols are they?" he said, turning back to Allie.

"I know exactly who these symbols belong to," she said as she brought the bag closer to her face for a moment and studied it. She lowered the bag and looked up at Dale. "A secret society."

CHAPTER NINETEEN

THE GRIZZLY LOOKED across his desk, and though the man sitting across from him hadn't introduced himself, he knew exactly who he was. There wasn't a bit of doubt in his mind.

"May I call you Jesse?" the Grizzly said.

Jesse James sneered. "That would be just fine."

He looked just as the rumors had described him. Bright blond hair, parted and cut short on the sides. An out-of-date look. A hairstyle of the 1950s. Or the Nazis. He wore a button-up shirt with a simple pattern, and it was wrinkled, unkempt, like he'd seen physical activity that night. Which made sense. His build was average, as were his looks. Physically, he was kind of plain. Not unpleasant looking. But still the Grizzly found him repulsive. It was the eyes. The way he looked at him. The Grizzly had been around long enough to recognize racism. And this guy had it bad. Even though the man was sitting in his office in the most congenial of manners, there was no hiding his eyes. He was brimming with hate. He was eaten up with it.

Since most of the drug deaths had been black folk, people

had been saying for some time that James was out to kill as many blacks as he could. And while the Grizzly couldn't deny the facts—and he did believe that race must be part of the equation—to this point he had refused to believe that anyone would invest massive resources with the sole hope of getting as many people hooked and dying as possible. There had to be a financial component. It only made logical sense.

But as he looked at the man now, face-to-face, man-to-man, he realized that he had been wrong. None of this had been based in logic. Only emotion. There was not but evil staring back at him. Jesse James was indeed on a quest. A mission. A mission of death.

He was a formidable opponent. This conversation was going to be a challenge. The Grizzly would need to plan his moves carefully. Like a chess game.

"Normally when someone comes here without an appointment, I turn them away, Jesse," the Grizzly said. "But how could I deny someone who announced himself as a knight?" He picked up one of the chess pieces from his desk—a knight. He broadened his smile a bit.

"I *am* a knight," Jesse James said. His voice was cold and steady with a thick Southern accent. "And my organization is here to reach an agreement with you."

"Why now? Why after all this subterfuge do you come to me in the middle of the night trying to make a deal?"

"Because it's time for my operations in the city to expand, and you hold all the power in this side of town."

"You don't honestly think I'll work with you. Your shit's killing people. That's just bad business."

James laughed at him. "You're misunderstanding. This isn't a business opportunity. I'm giving you the option of not being destroyed. Here's the deal. Give me what I want, and I'll stay out of your neighborhoods. If you don't, we'll bury you. Send a wave of our stuff into your turf. You won't sell another dime bag. There won't be one junkie left standing to sell to. I think you've seen what we're capable of."

James' words were ominous. But true. He wouldn't be able to take a hit from James' drugs. "And what is it you want from me?"

James sneered again. He knew he had the upper hand. "Two things. First, information. Your territory is up here north of the French Quarter. With the Saint Louis Cemeteries. You have dozens of dealers, hundreds of junkies crawling over this area. *Someone* will be able to tell me where to find this symbol in the cemeteries."

He reached into his pocket, took out a paper, and tossed it onto the Grizzly's desk. He didn't hand it to him. He made the Grizzly pick it up. A power move.

The Grizzly looked at the sketch on the paper. "A moon?"

James nodded. "That's right. And I need to know immediately. Tonight."

"And the second thing?"

James narrowed his eyes. "Cooperation. Rumor has it a couple cops came by here the other day. Big wigs. Feds, I figure. I also figure you're helping them out. I got a call right before I came here. They nearly caught one of our guys. Somehow they knew *exactly* where the deal was going down. Now, maybe they heard this through the grapevine, but I find it pretty coincidental that this happened the same day they met with you. From now on, you keep up appearances with them. And you report to us. Understand?"

The Grizzly hated giving up this power to another man. But he saw little other alternative. "Seems to me that it's in my best business interests to help you out in any way I can," he said and put the knight back on his desk. "This organization of yours ... if you're a knight, who's the king?"

James just scoffed.

"What do you call yourselves?" the Grizzly said.

James stood up. "You find out where that moon is. You got an hour."

He left.

CHAPTER TWENTY

LUANNE'S BREATH WAS SHORT, and her heart beat rapidly. She didn't know why she was doing it, why she was there.

She was at the desk in her bedroom. Dylan's desk. She'd been told never to use it. But there she was anyway. Sitting in the chair behind the desk, looking at the items covering its surface.

It was pitch-black outside the window, and the light sitting on the desktop cast a warm glow. She had the trailer to herself. Dylan and the boys were gone. They'd left for a quick run to a nearby gas station that was open late. She only had about ten minutes.

It wasn't often that she got time entirely to herself. She was supposed to be cooking a snack. There was a pot of popcorn on the stovetop that she'd started shortly before the guys left. It was only now starting to pop. She hated that Dylan let the boys stay up late to watch television with them like this. Especially Tyler. He was only five. But at least it was some semblance of family time. And at least Dylan was including Caleb.

While Luanne would normally use any small reprieve of

solitude for something personal—listening to music, maybe reading a few pages—she was using this bit of time for something else. Something more productive.

Because she couldn't stop thinking about the bizarre list of city names and creepy drawings that she'd found in the car the other night.

She looked through the papers on the top corner of the desk while the popping sounds of the popcorn grew louder from the other side of the trailer. Dylan wasn't a tidy person, so the paperwork and other items were scattered haphazardly. This would make it more difficult for him to tell that she had looked through things. Or, the more she thought about it, maybe it would do just the opposite. Maybe Dylan's system was organized chaos, and he'd be able to tell if one single item was slightly out of place.

She couldn't bear thinking about the repercussions. So she pushed the thoughts from her mind.

There were invoices. Receipts. Shipping statements. Everything related to his work. It all seemed legitimate, but she continued to remind herself of the bizarre symbols. Something was going on here. She knew it.

Then she saw her cousin's name. Jesse Richter. Written on a paper with a list of other names she didn't recognize. She did a double-take. While she knew that Dylan and Jesse had been spending more time together lately, she had no clue why his name would be written on a piece of paper among the business items on the desk. She pulled the paper out a bit. Jesse's name was—

There was movement in the window outside. She looked up. Headlights in the darkness. It was the Corvair. They were back already. The car was at the end of the road.

Just like that, her few minutes of solitude were almost over. If she was going to find something, she needed to find it now.

The popcorn was popping faster now, frantic noise matching the pace with which she was going through the documents.

She peeled back the papers covering the one with Jesse's name. There was nothing labeling it. It was just a list of names, about twenty of them, with Jesse's being at the top, and they had been written in different colors of ink, as though the list had been added to over time. It was yet another perplexing piece of information—another confusing list—but it was not the smoking gun she was hoping for. She put it back.

She sifted through the paperwork. More receipts. Some sort of voucher. But nothing related to that strange list of cities in the car, the list that she'd been thinking of almost constantly since she saw it.

Outside, the Corvair was about to turn onto the long path leading up to the trailer. She moved to the side, getting out of view of the window. The sound of the popcorn was rapid, incessant.

There had to be something there. Something that would shed some light. She knew there was something bizarre to that list and the symbols. She needed something concrete.

And then she found it.

A map of the Gulf South. Hand-drawn, clearly traced out of an encyclopedia or atlas. There were names written on the map in Dylan's handwriting, in pencil. Location names, written in their respective positions on the map. They were the places that had been on the list in the car: Pensacola, Naval Live Oaks, New Orleans, Marianna.

And next to each name was a small, simple drawing. The same drawings that had been on the list. They were like symbols. New Orleans had been without a symbol on the list, but it had one on the map: a crescent moon. With stars on it. Dylan had put a big question mark next to it.

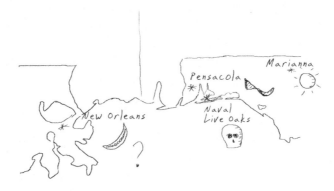

There were places where he'd written other things on the map. They'd been erased. She leaned in close, squinted. Other city names. Other drawings.

Light shined in the window. Headlights. The car was pulling up, stopping. There was the squeal of the brakes.

Rosemary Beach. Dothan. De Soto National Forest. Locations in the region, all of them erased. She looked closely at one of the places that wasn't erased, Marianna, and saw that it had been written multiple times. Written down, erased, and written again. And again.

It was like he was discovering places ...

Finding locations. Second-guessing and then confirming his work.

Outside the car door shut.

She jumped. The intrigue had made her forget herself for a moment. She would have to hurry. She stuffed the map back where it had been and headed to the front of the trailer, back to the popcorn at the stove, just as the hinges on the door squeaked.

Dylan and the boys stepped in. Tyler and Caleb were full of giggly energy. In their hands was the candy they'd gone to the gas station to get. They ran to the living room. Dylan stepped toward her, his boots stomping on the floor.

"Popcorn ready?"

Luanne nodded. "Just about, babe."

Dylan sniffed the air. "Smells burnt."

"I forgot about it for a minute."

Dylan looked her up and down. "Why are you breathing hard?"

"I had to run to get it," she said. "I was in the bathroom."

He just looked at her.

She smiled. "Let's watch the show."

Luanne was happy. While there were two nagging feelings whispering at her—the unease she felt about Dylan's mysterious activities and her tension that the boys were up so late eating candy and watching TV—she felt content to be having some family time. She was on the couch with Caleb, and Dylan sat in the chair with Tyler in his lap. The lights were out. There was only the glow of the television.

The main character in the show said something funny, and Dylan laughed loudly. He thrust his hand into the popcorn bowl, which sat on the table between the chair and the couch, and took out a big handful. He offered some to Tyler then stuffed some into his mouth.

Luanne looked at him. She was going to get a bit more information, but she needed to play it casual. "I saw that one of those guys you were talking to tonight was Mick Henderson. What's a guy like that doing with your business?"

Dylan slowly turned to her. The light from the TV bounced off his face, his unkempt beard. He frowned. "What did you just ask me?"

She paused for a moment before answering, She had to be

careful. "I mean, he's one of the biggest names in the region, and I just wouldn't know what someone in his field would need with a pharmaceutical shipping firm."

Dylan narrowed his eyes. There was a pause. The screeching sound of tires came from the television. "That's none of your business."

Luanne gave him a smile. "I'm just proud of you, baby. That's all."

Dylan didn't answer. He stared at her. She smiled again and looked back at the television. She could feel his eyes still upon her.

Caleb leaned over to her. "Momma?"

A break in the tension. She felt a wave of relief.

"Yes, baby?"

"I'm hungry."

"Have some popcorn." She reached for the bowl.

"No, I'm *hungry* hungry."

She smiled at him. "Okay, you can have my leftovers from Bello. You like spaghetti."

"Yeah!"

Dylan turned to them. "The boy's had dinner *and* candy *and* popcorn. He'll be happy with what he gets. And what are you talking about? Bello? You said you two were getting coffee."

Luanne had driven into town that afternoon to visit with her friend Maria.

"I haven't seen her in three months," she said. "We thought we'd eat instead."

"So you drove all the way into Pensacola *and* you bought lunch. And you weren't gonna tell me?"

Luanne could tell when Dylan's anger was rising. And there were few things that made him angrier than things he perceived as disrespect. She again needed to play it safe, be diplomatic. "I wasn't trying to hide nothing from you. It just slipped my mind, baby. Honest."

"I don't know why you were eating pasta, Luanne. God knows you don't need it." He pointed at Caleb. "Twinkle-toes here isn't getting it either. Tyler can have it. You want some spaghetti, boy?"

Tyler nodded vigorously.

Dylan watched Luanne for a moment. There was intensity in that stare. Luanne felt it bore into her. The anger was rising.

"So was it a good visit, at least?" he said.

Luanne smiled. Maybe she'd been premature. He couldn't be too angry at her if he was asking how the visit went. "It was so great catching up with her. She's taking classes at PJC, you know. And she's still in touch with all the people we went to high school with. She gave me the lowdown on how many of them—"

"Wait," Dylan said, frowning. "The 'lowdown'?"

The anger was still there. In his eyes. More tension. She realized that she was starting to breath harder.

"Yeah. You know, the 'information.' The 'scoop.'"

Dylan smirked. A disgusted smirk. The look he gave her when he wanted her to know just how worthless she was. This was usually followed by a slap to the face. "She gave you the 'lowdown,' did she, Luanne? That's how you're talking now? Like some damn city hippie?"

Calm him down. That's the only thing she could try to do now. She knew where this was going. "It doesn't mean nothing. It's just a word. It's just silly."

"You're right. It is silly. Which is why I don't want you hanging around people like her." He gestured at Caleb and Tyler. "See, boys, this here is my mistake. I've let your momma down." He looked at Tyler on his lap. "It's time for a little lesson. You want to help Daddy out, big guy?"

Tyler nodded.

Something terrible was going to happen. Something worse than a slap. Luanne could feel it. Dylan had that look in his eye. A look of menace. And glee.

"Good," Dylan said. "Luanne, come here."

Luanne didn't want to move. She wanted to stay right there on the couch. With Caleb. Safe.

"I said, come here, Luanne!"

She stood up. If she just did what he said, maybe he'd reconsider whatever it was he had planned. She stepped over to him.

"Now lean down," he said.

Luanne began to understand what her husband had in mind. "Dylan, no. He's my little boy."

"*Lean down.*"

Luanne bent over. She began to cry. She tried not to, but that just made her cry harder.

Dylan craned his neck around her and called out to Caleb. "Now pay attention, sissy boy. You're gonna learn a thing or two from your baby brother." He settled back in his seat and got his face right up next to Tyler's. "Now you're gonna slap Momma. I'm gonna let you do it this time."

Tyler chuckled, hid his face in his hands, embarrassed.

"Now reach back."

Tyler pulled his little arm back.

"No, waaaaay back."

"Dylan, no. Please."

His face looked up at her. A slight redness to his skin. Hate buried in his eyes. "Shut up, bitch." He turned back to Tyler. "You have to hit her hard. You want what's best for your momma, don't ya? Good. Hard. Like the way you hit that pillow of yours sometimes. Grr!"

Tyler imitated him. "Grr!"

Dylan laughed. "Atta boy. Now ... *go!*"

Tyler slapped her. A small spot of pain on her cheek. Her face snapped to the side.

Her boy had hit her.

Dylan had used him against her. Humiliation. Disrespect. Degradation.

She stood up, grabbed her cheek, cried openly. "Oh, Dylan. How could you? He's my boy."

She turned and ran away, sobbing.

His voice came from behind her. "Boohoo! That's right. Poor baby. Boohoo, bitch!"

She ran into the bathroom. The thin door thudded shut as she closed it behind her. She turned to the mirror but didn't look into it. Her face was in her hands. Sobs. Chest heaving, hurting. Her cheeks felt wet, hot against her hands. Tears moistened the spaces between her fingers.

From the other end of the trailer, Dylan's taunts continued. "Boohoo, bitch! Boohoo!"

She thought about Tyler. His face. Her boy. He was getting big. Heavy. She still picked him up occasionally, but she didn't carry him anymore. He was getting too big for that. She missed carrying him. It wasn't that long ago that she'd carried him inside her. Life in her stomach. Life that she'd loved before it had even come to be.

And Dylan had used that against her.

"Poor baby! Poor little crybaby bitch!"

She took a deep breath. *Stop crying.* Another deep breath. Her body still quivered, but the crying was over. Slowly she pulled her face out of her hands. Looked up. And saw herself in the mirror.

The verbal assault from the other end of the trailer had ended. There was relative silence. Just the muffled sound of the television.

Her eyes were bloodshot. Mascara stained her lower

eyelids, lines of it running down her cheeks, which were wet with tears. Her body shook. Another deep breath.

This had happened because of two words. Because she'd been too cool. Too exposed to the outside world. *The lowdown.*

Luanne thought of the times Dylan had slapped her. They were beyond count. She could take it. But this was different. He'd involved her boy. Her child. And that hurt worse than any of the times he'd put hands on her.

Usually, they'd only been slaps. Shoves. Squeezes to the arms that left bruises. But there were a few times ...

Her attention moved away from the face staring back at her as her eyes traced down the mirror to her blouse. It was a faux-silk polyester. Green. Large collar. Button-up. A bit of her chest was visible, just below the throat.

Her fingers moved to the cloth, pulled it to the side, revealing her right collarbone. There was a scar there. He'd done more than slap her that night, and the skin had split. She'd thought that the bone broke too, but luckily it had not. The scar had healed wide. No stitches. Dylan hadn't let her go to the doctor. They used butterfly bandages to pull the edges of the wound together.

She continued pulling her shirt aside.

Her shoulder showed itself. Another scar there. They'd been on the trailer's porch. He'd hit her so many times and so hard that she fell over, whacking her shoulder against the metal railing. She had crawled away from him, on her stomach, down the steps and onto the drive. He'd grabbed her ankles. Pulled her back. Laughing. Rocks had dug into her stomach, arms.

Her hand pulled away, and the blouse fell back over her shoulder. There were more scars to find. Some were on her ribs. From an incident behind the barn. She began to unbutton the blouse.

And stopped.

Her arms wrapped around herself. And she looked herself in the eye again.

The arms squeezed in tight, comforting, reassuring, and her hands caressed her torso, finding all the areas, all the memories of times when things had gotten their worst. Healing coursed through her fingertips.

She didn't want to believe that every man was like this, and a memory of her life before Dylan reminded her that they weren't. Alec Corber. Luanne was a faithful woman, and she felt guilty every time she thought about Alec. But she only thought about him after the times Dylan had truly given her a beating. Or, in this case, when he'd given her an emotional beating by using her child against her.

She let the thoughts enter.

Alec. His hands, so different than Dylan's. Strong like Dylan's but a strength that felt good when they touched her. Hands that moved so gently over her body the two times they had been naked together. Hands. On her face. Brushing the hair from her eyes. Dylan would pull her hair, not look at her. Alec would gaze right back. His brown eyes. Lips so gentle. Saying kind things. Dylan would say swear words, squeeze her nipples until she cried out for him to stop. Alec's hands. Coarse, callused. He was a mechanic. Hands that never hurt her. Coarse. And strong. On her thighs. Up her thighs. Holding her arms down gently. Her hair had gotten in her eyes again. He brushed it away. Locked eyes with her. Told her she was beautiful.

Alec's hands.

Her own hands were still wrapped around her sides, and she could almost believe they were Alec's as they moved along her torso.

Then she heard the television. She was back. In the trailer.

She thought again of the phrase that had caused this. Two words. *The lowdown.*

There was another meaning for the word *lowdown.* It meant *mean.* And that's what Dylan was. A lowdown, mean, evil man. Maybe she hadn't noticed when he gave her the scar on her collarbone or when he left the other scar on her shoulder. But when he used one of her boys as a tool of cruelty against her ... now she knew for sure.

And she wasn't going to have it.

Not for her and sure as hell not for her boys.

Dylan was lowdown and rotten. And not just with her. Not just at home. He was up to something—with his list of strange locations with creepy drawings and meetings with people like Mick Henderson.

Luanne was going figure out what Dylan was doing.

CHAPTER TWENTY-ONE

JESSE WALKED through the darkened cemetery of above-ground, crumbling crypts. He held a flashlight. Its light bounced off the tombs, revealing macabre designs and long-forgotten dates, casting eerie shadows.

He stopped and examined one of the tombs. At the top was a moon decoration carved into the stone. It was a full moon. A circle with smaller circles within. Wrong. He moved on.

According to the information he'd gotten from the Grizzly, this was the correct row. Now he just had to find the right tomb. He saw another moon shape and stopped. It was a crescent moon, thin, with little star designs down its length. And unlike the last moon he'd examined—which protruded from the stone in a large, central position—this one was chiseled into the stone, and it was inconspicuous, only a couple inches across, hidden away in the upper-right corner.

Jesse smiled. This was it. Now, even if he had made a colossal mistake with the Madame Gertrude situation, Dylan would be ecstatic that Jesse had found the final symbol. Jesse breathed a sigh of relief. This would set everything right.

But he wouldn't tell Dylan that he'd joined forces with the Grizzly. Not yet. Not until he found out more about the cops.

He took out a notebook and wrote down the names, dates, and inscriptions on the tomb then did a quick sketch of the symbol. He looked to the end of the row and counted the number of tombs, wrote it down, then counted the number of rows and jotted that down as well. He turned off the flashlight and stuffed it in his pocket along with the notebook. He turned to leave.

The cemetery was dark. A lot of people would pay good money to be in his shoes right now—strolling in one of the famous Saint Louis Cemeteries at night. He'd had to climb the wall to get in. The gates were locked at night. He walked up the main gravel road that went through the center of the cemetery, heading back toward the wall.

Two figures emerged from the tombs. They approached. Jesse stopped.

Blacks. Both male. Destitute clothing. Both of them large. One of them incredibly tall.

"Cemetery's closed," the tall one said. "Didn't you hear?"

The second one was fatter with a mustache and a nasally voice. "Gate's locked. How'd you get in?"

Jesse hated to give them the validation of a response, but he knew he was in a precarious situation. He summoned his abilities again. Time to transform. To radiate simpleness. Purity.

"Aw, jeez. I get caught for everything," he said with smile, looking away guiltily. "I didn't get a chance to visit earlier, and it's my last night in town. So I hopped the wall."

"Yeah? Well, you hopped right into our home, man. We live here," the tall one said.

"And don't much care for intruders neither," his partner said and pulled back his jacket, revealing a revolver.

Jesse looked at the gun and paused for just a moment—before springing into action.

He'd been well trained in martial arts. When he first started, he'd hated the idea of studying Eastern philosophical nonsense. All the funny letters on the walls and the backwards customs. Bowing and all that. But he knew that they were the most efficient and well received forms of hand-to-hand combat. So in his quest to prepare himself for the war he knew was coming, he had studied karate, jiujitsu, and tae kwon do. And he knew ways of disarming a man.

He spun on the fat one, who had drawn his gun, and lunged toward him, grabbing the arm with the gun. He twisted. The gun fired into the ground, spraying gravel on them before it dropped from his hand. Jesse lowered himself and used the man's bodyweight to flip him over his shoulder. He landed on his back in the gravel.

Arms grabbed Jesse from behind. The taller one. Jesse was in a full nelson. He rammed his head back into the man's face and used the moment while the man was stunned to pull himself out of his grasp. He ducked under the man's shoulder, pulling his hand with him as he went. He now had the man's arm twisted behind his back. With one swift motion, he flung the man over his extended leg, sending him into one of the nearby tombs. His skull *cracked* against the stone. Skin split. Blood gushed out. He collapsed into a motionless lump. He'd hit hard. Broken neck, most likely.

Jesse didn't hesitate. The gun. Where was it?

To the side. A few feet away. Moonlight glistened off the barrel.

Jesse grabbed it, pointed it down at the other man on the ground a few feet away from him. The fat one. The man put his hands up, looking absurd as he did so, bloodied and lying in the gravel.

A look came across the man's face, a look of realization that overpowered his fear. "Jesse James?"

Jesse grinned. Took aim. Right at the man's chest. His heart.

A noise behind him. A short burst from a police siren. Blue lights bounced off the tombs.

He turned. A cop car was on the other side of the gate. A figure stepped out.

Jesse fired the gun into the man on the ground then sprinted away into the darkened maze of tombs.

CHAPTER TWENTY-TWO

"THE KNIGHTS OF THE GOLDEN CIRCLE," Allie said. "That's the name of the secret society who uses these markings." She handed Dale a book.

Percy leaned over Dale's shoulder and looked at the cover.

An Authentic Exposition of the K.G.C., Knights of the Golden Circle

It had the old book smell and looked ancient and delicate in Dale's hands. As Dale flipped open the cover, Percy saw a bizarre title page full of lavish fonts, creepy skeletal drawings, and an image of a group of men in matching clothing, standing in a circle around a lone man under a domed structure with a sun behind it.

Weird.

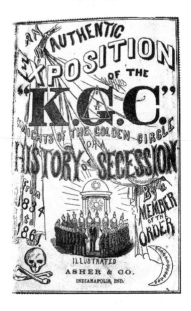

They were in the office that the NOPD had provided them for the duration of the assignment as a central hub for their task force. This was at the District 1 Station, which was on Rampart Street, the dividing line between Districts 1 and 8, the French Quarter. Since nearly all their activity had taken place in these two districts, it was a perfect location.

The room was about twelve feet squared, no exterior windows. There was a single door and a window that faced the main office space. They had been keeping the bent metal blinds shut. There was a desk to the right—sturdy, metal, painted green. The table in the center was surrounded by four chairs. The linoleum was dirty. The walls needed painting. The lighting was fluorescent. On the back wall was a large cork board, the surface of which was covered with papers and dominated by two large maps: one of New Orleans and one of the Gulf South region, each dotted with pins.

Dale and Percy sat on one side of the table. Allie was on the other. In the center of the table were the bags of Jesse

James' drugs, and to the sides were large piles of books and stacks of photocopied papers—the results of Marty Rhode's impromptu research session at the Library of Congress in D.C. Some of the materials, like the book Dale held in his hand, were originals, but much of it had to be copied. There were boxes along the walls filled with yet more materials. Rhodes had been thorough.

Dale flipped through the book ... and a slight smile came to his face. Dale was always grinning about something. Smartasses were like that. Percy had spent so much time around him that he could decipher all those little looks. This one had narrowed eyes and a tinge of holier-than-thou-ness. It was a skeptical grin. Dale thought the book was bullshit.

And as he looked at the pages while Dale flipped through them, Percy could sympathize with those sentiments. He picked up a few words here and there—things about handshakes and rituals. And there were images, too: symbols, numbers, and the like.

Percy knew that Dale had seen a lot of hocus-pocus conspiracy theories in his time with the BEI, but he had to keep Dale from getting too carried away with his cynicism. Even if there was no truth to the Knights of the Golden Circle, this didn't change the fact that it looked like the people they were chasing did believe in the group and were emulating it.

Dale closed the book, rapped a knuckle on the cover, and pointed at Percy. "Told you Arty Marty would come through."

"And I told you we needed to bring in Allie," Percy said, giving her a reverential nod.

She smiled at him.

Dale opened the book again and examined one of the drawings more closely. "So, Allie, what … is this?"

"The KGC," Allie said. "A secret society during the Civil War. Plans of partial world domination. They originally wanted to create a slaveholding empire from the American South, through Mexico, and all the way into the northern part of South America. A golden circle."

"During the Civil War?" Dale said. "This book's publication date is 1861. That's the year the war began."

Allie nodded. "That's what I mean when I say that their *original* goal was to create the golden slaveholding circle. When the states divided, the KGC changed their mission and affiliated themselves with the Confederacy. They were the South's secret society. Meetings in barns. Initiation ceremonies. Symbols and handshakes. Very clandestine. They were all over, infiltrating the North."

"Wait a minute," Dale said with another one of his grins. "Now I remember why those symbols on the bags look familiar. You told me about the KGC when we dated. You and Ronan were looking into them. Isn't this the group that's supposed to have buried gold all over the country? Something about symbols, too, if I remember right. Symbols in cemeteries that were supposed to lead to the gold—all these crazy coots with metal detectors and treasure maps out looking for it."

Allie gave him a glare that would wilt a houseplant. Percy had spent considerable time with Allie during his first assignment with Dale, so he knew her well enough to tell when she was genuinely perturbed. And Allie was pissed.

"My father and I were not 'crazy coots with metal detectors,'" she said. "We were legitimate treasure hunters. I know you never respected what he did, but he took it very seriously."

Sometimes you just had to shake your head at Dale. For as smart as the guy was, his people skills were infantile, and he could be completely oblivious to the damage that his big mouth inflicted on others. Percy was sure that Dale hadn't meant to insult the memory of Allie's deceased father, and by the kindly tone of his response, it was clear that he was trying to immediately backpedal. "I heard about Ronan. I'm so sorry, Allie. He was a good man."

"You sure didn't seem to think so at the time. You said the work he did should've been left to archaeologists."

"And I still believe that. But that doesn't change the fact that he was a great man."

She took in a long breath, let it out, and nodded. "Thank you."

There was a tap at the door. Dale stood and opened it. It was Detective Snyder, his sleeves rolled up, tie loosened.

"She's here now," he said and motioned back toward the main office. "I want you to see this first, though." He handed Dale a piece of paper. "We just got a call. Anonymous source. They gave us this info."

Percy stepped over to them.

"What in the world?" Dale said. He handed the paper to Percy.

It was a scribbled list of locations on a small sheet of paper with an NOPD logo at the top:

Pensacola
Naval Live Oaks
New Orleans
Marianna

Snyder shrugged. "It was a woman. She said she wanted to get this list of places to the people investigating the drug deaths. That's all she'd say." He stepped out.

Percy scanned the list. "New Orleans and Pensacola are two of our four cities. Never heard of these other two. Are they on the coast too?"

Dale walked over to the regional map on the opposite wall.

"Naval Live Oaks is a part of the NPS. Gulf Islands National Seashore. Riiiiiight..." He searched the Pensacola, Florida, area of the map then found the location and poked it with his finger. "Here. It's a nature preserve. It's got a few hiking trails. Live oak timber was used in shipbuilding, all the way back to the eighteenth century. Tough wood. That's how Old Ironsides—the USS *Constitution*—got her nickname." Dale's finger was on the peninsula that lay between Pensacola and Santa Rosa Island, the barrier island where Pensacola Beach was located. He searched the map again. "As to Marianna ... I have no idea where that is."

A voice came from the doorway.

"Excuse me, gentlemen." It was Snyder again. With him was a woman wearing an ornate dress. Madame Gertrude had arrived. She was in her thirties, on the short side, heavyset, black. She looked bewildered, out of place.

"Come in. Please. Have a seat," Dale said and waved her into the room. He and Percy returned to the table.

Madame Gertrude took the chair beside Allie and smiled at her. Snyder leaned against the doorframe.

"I'm Special Agent Dale Conley with the DOJ. This is my associate Percy Gordon, DEA, and our expert consultant, Allison Blair. We're told that you believe you've had an encounter with Jesse James."

"I don't just think I did," she said. "I know it was him."

"Tell us about it," Percy said.

She settled into her seat, relaxed a bit more. "He came into my shop on Bourbon Street. I have video for you. He gave me a real weird vibe from the moment I saw him. He was about six-foot tall, white, blond hair, light brown eyes."

Percy scribbled down her description as she spoke. Everything she said matched the other descriptions they'd gotten.

A scratchy sound from the other side of the room. The radio on Snyder's belt came alive. He was still leaning against the doorframe, and he jumped at the sound. He turned the volume down and put the radio to his ear.

"He didn't try to buy anything," Madame Gertrude continued. "Wasn't interested in getting a reading. He just came right up to me and started asking about symbols."

Allie came to attention, gave Dale a look, and then turned to Madame Gertrude. "What kind of symbols?"

"Well, specifically he was looking for information about symbols in the Saint Louis Cemeteries."

Allie looked at Dale again, a wry twinkle in her eye. *I told you so.* "Cemeteries, huh?"

Madame Gertrude nodded. "Yes, and by the end of the conversation, he asked me about a specific symbol he thought might be in the cemeteries. A moon shape."

Allie reached across the table and grabbed the book she'd given Dale, flipped a few pages, and handed it to Madame Gertrude, tapping an image with her finger.

Percy could see the image Allie was indicating. It was the moon he had seen earlier.

Allie kept her finger on the page. "Do you think there could be any symbols like this moon in the Saint Louis Cemeteries?"

"Oh, lord, yes," Madame Gertrude said. "There are designs all over those cemeteries."

Snyder spoke up. "Fellas, sorry to interrupt, but you two need to get the hell out of here. Right now."

Dale leaned forward. "What?"

"Your guy's supposed to be stalking the Saint Louis Cemeteries, right?" He held up his radio. "We just had shots fired at Saint Louis Cemetery No. 2. That's three blocks from here."

CHAPTER TWENTY-THREE

IT HAD RAINED a bit earlier in the evening, and the pavement was slippery as Dale sprinted up to the wall. Percy had fallen behind again. The poor guy. He'd surely done more running that night than he'd done the rest of the year combined.

The wall encircling Saint Louis Cemetery No. 2 was about ten feet tall and made of brick, which was weathered, stained, crumbling. As Dale ran up to it, he saw a metal gate, chained and padlocked. A patrol car was pulled right up to the gate, its lights flashing. The cop had created a stepping stool with the hood of his car to help him clear the gate. Smart.

Dale ran up to the car, hopped on the hood, and flung himself over the top of the gate. He landed with a thud on the gravel beyond. He heard Percy behind him, out of breath, climbing onto the car. In front of Dale was a straight path, wide enough for a single car, that cut down the center of the cemetery. On the opposite end of the road was another gate matching the one he had just jumped. Through that gate he could see a city street and beyond that another block of the cemetery with its own gated wall.

Percy landed with a grunt. He stepped up beside Dale.

The road was lined on either side with the famous above-ground tombs of New Orleans. Crumbling forms of stone and brick. Some bone white. Others dark. Box-shaped structures with slots for bodies. Little wrought iron fences. Tokens left by tourists. Saint Louis was renowned for its macabre appeal, the eerie final resting place for an eclectic and varied group of people in a city that was equally varied and eclectic. The tombs' boxy shapes made them look like miniature buildings, giving the cemeteries their nickname: the Cities of the Dead.

It was dark, but the numerous streetlights gave everything a tinge of orange. The air was so thick you could see the moisture particles floating under the lights. To the right, just beyond the cemetery, I-10 loomed, twenty feet in the sky on big, round columns. Before they jumped the gate, Dale had seen a mass of homeless people under the highway. A shanty town. There was the constant sound of high-speed traffic on wet concrete.

Further up on the road were two bodies. Homeless men by the looks of the clothing. Clearly dead. One lay right in the middle of the road. Another was crumpled against one of the tombs. A wide streak of blood ran down the side of the tomb to the body, glistening in the muted light.

Dale drew his Smith & Wesson Model 36 and yelled out into the cemetery. "Officer! This is Special Agent Dale Conley. Two federal agents are entering the cemetery. We're armed. In plain clothes."

Snyder had radioed that he and Percy would be arriving on foot, but Dale still had to be safe and announce their arrival.

Percy drew his own weapon—a Colt Python, 4-inch—and the two of them held perfectly still, listened. Sounds of a struggle, echoing strangely off the tombs. Somewhere ahead.

Dale and Percy ran toward the noise.

It was coming from the left. Dale turned, off the main

path. He came to a corner, one of hundreds in the place. With its towering tombs, the cemetery was a giant maze. Like the Greek Labyrinth. Dale just had to find the minotaur.

So many corners. He thought back to his training at the FBI Academy. How to turn a corner, how to clear a room. He looked back to give Percy a signal. And he wasn't there. Somehow he'd lost him. Dale was alone.

More footsteps. A grunt. He peered forward. Couldn't see anything. It was darker here than it had been on the main road. He plastered himself against the nearest tomb. The stone was cold against his back. He tightened his grip on his gun. Listened. The sounds were impossible to track, bouncing off the walls and angles and varying materials, getting absorbed into the thick, moist air.

Dale couldn't remain stationary. He had to move. He cleared a corner. There was an empty path in front of him. Just tombs. Crumbling brick and cement. Open holes where coffins had been.

More corners. More paths to clear. Tombs and stone. The sound of footsteps. Percy? The cop? Jesse James?

He turned another corner. And saw a form. On the ground. A body. It was the cop. Dale could just make out his cap lying a couple feet from his head. The man was still. But breathing.

More footsteps. Someone was running. To his left.

Dale threw caution to the wind, turned, and ran through the tombs. The noise had sounded far away. As he ran, he saw for just a moment the body of the homeless man on the road. His eyes were open. A gunshot wound to the chest.

Dale sprinted to the back wall. Then he saw movement. A person. Someone was climbing the wall. A few feet away from Dale. The man reached the top of the wall and turned his head.

They looked right at each other.

It was him.

Jesse James.

Blond. Six-foot tall. A button-up shirt, sleeves rolled up. A pair of slacks.

In that briefest of moments when their eyes were locked, Dale felt the hair on his arms stand up. Palpable negativity poured out of the man's gaze. Hate. Rage. Rot.

James went to jump over the side, and Dale grabbed his foot and pulled viciously. They landed in a jumbled mess on the ground. Dale's temple smacked into a stone. Sharp pain. James pulled out a gun, aimed. Dale grabbed his wrist, smashed it into the edge of a nearby tomb. The gun clattered to the ground.

There was a flurry of motion and impacts, scrambling on the ground, shuffling gravel and stone. Dale elbowed James in the shoulder then took a punch to the ribs. And another to the back of his head. He fell back, and James slipped out of his grasp.

Dale was back on his feet. Jesse James was nowhere to be seen. Disappeared. Back into the dark hell surrounding him. Dale stood still, held his breath. And listened again.

Two sets of footsteps.

One set came from his left. Dale positioned himself beside a tomb, gulped down a breath, and whipped around the corner, gun drawn.

Another gun. Pointing at him. A Colt Python. It was Percy. Thirty feet away.

Dale exhaled. Both men lowered their weapons. Dale pointed back into the maze of tombs where the other footsteps had come from, moving his arm in an arc. He then patted himself on the chest and pointed to the right. Percy nodded. He knew what Dale intended. They were going to put the squeeze on Jesse James. Encircle him. Tighten the net.

Dale repositioned his fingers around the grip of his Smith. His hands were sweating. One more deep breath, and he plunged into the next, darker row of tombs. A figure cut across the gap in the distance, the silhouette illuminated for just a moment before disappearing again. Percy, getting himself into position. Another noise, farther ahead. Their quarry.

The wall appeared before Dale, a few feet ahead. He looked down another gap between the tombs, cleared another corner. Another fleeting glimpse of Percy. More footsteps. Crunching gravel. Only a few feet away. Dale turned a corner.

And there was Percy. Gun drawn. Smiling. Because in front of him was Jesse James.

James spun around. Saw Dale. His eyes went wide.

Dale leveled his Smith at him. Their gazes met once more. Those burning eyes.

James' shoulders dropped slightly. His chest heaved as he gasped for air. The chase was over. Hands shaking. Quivering rage. A look of utter, forsaken, and complete hatred, like the fingers of some invisible demon were at work, twisting and contorting the man's face.

It was a chilling look. And it made Dale's heart sink knowing that a human being could get that dark.

But there was no way Dale was going to let James know that he'd gotten to him. So Dale just said, "Gotcha, you son of a bitch."

CHAPTER TWENTY-FOUR

DYLAN SAT in the living room of his trailer. He leaned forward in his orange, tattered armchair, his elbows on his knees, and got closer to the television set. To his right, the kids were making noise, distracting him.

"Quiet!"

He heard them scamper off.

On the screen was a press conference. A black man with a mustache, wearing a suit. The bottom of the screen read *Percy Gordon, Drug Enforcement Administration*. It was the top story in the ten o'clock news, and given the urgency with which the newscaster had announced it, something just told Dylan that it was related to the drugs. Jesse Richter had shit the bed again. He just knew it. But when Gordon started talking about the symbols on the bags, Dylan recognized that his upcoming issues were going to be a lot more difficult than just reprimanding Jesse. A lot.

"... and *any* bag with these markings, regardless of the contents, should be considered dangerous," Gordon was saying. He motioned to the side, and the camera followed his hand to a projector screen that displayed a magnified image of one of the sets of markings Dylan's men had been scoring into the plastic bags. "Anyone with further information about these markings or the drugs in question should contact the New Orleans Police Department immediately. Are there any questions?"

There was a bustling reaction off-screen, reporters yelling out to Gordon. Arms raised from the bottom of the screen as they vied for Gordon's attention He pointed at one of them.

A female voice. "What do the symbols mean?"

"We have a team of experts analyzing the markings right now," Gordon said and looked out to the reporters for the next question. More hands raised, shouts of *Agent Gordon*. He pointed at another.

Dylan's phone rang. He knew who it was before he answered.

———

"I know, Henderson," Dylan said. "An absolute catastrophe."

"You're damn right it is," Henderson said. "This is the end of the operation as far as the investors are concerned. You realize that? We need to move fast if we're going to accomplish our own objective."

Dylan had already considered this. He and Henderson needed to move more than "fast." They needed to move immediately. "I have a plan. All these hillbilly investors and the knights are only in this thing to kill black people. Let's give them their big finale. Tomorrow night. Let them think they cut their losses. We'll use the Great Contingency."

There was a silence on the other end as Henderson thought it over. "Agreed. But what about us? The Great Contingency will end the KGC. And when the KGC ends, so does our cover. Has Jesse Richter found the last symbol?"

"He got it narrowed down to a specific Saint Louis Cemetery—No. 2. He was supposed to have confirmed with me earlier tonight. Never heard back. And none of my sentries in New Orleans have reported. I think they're covering for him. Jesse might've been caught."

There was a long exhale on the other end of the line. "So what the hell are we supposed to do now?"

"I'll handle Jesse," Dylan said. "It doesn't matter if he found the specific grave. All we really need to know is which of the Saint Louis Cemeteries the symbol was in. We know that now. I already checked the lines on the map. I know where to find the coordinates. It's right down the road. A cemetery in Pensacola. I'm going there first thing in the morning. At first light. I'll get us the coordinates."

"Even if you do find the coordinates, we still have to keep the main operation running until we can use them to find the location. If they caught Jesse Richter, this whole thing could come crashing down in a matter of hours."

Dylan smiled. Henderson was a major part of all this—both the KGC and his and Dylan's main objective. But he was rich. And sheltered. He hadn't gotten his hands dirty. He hadn't seen the coordination that Dylan had built into the KGC system he'd created, nor had he seen the baffling, child-like loyalty of his knights. "Don't worry. If the cops do have Jesse, they won't be able to hold onto him for long."

CHAPTER TWENTY-FIVE

THEY WALKED three-wide down the dark sidewalk, their feet crunching on the cement—Percy to the left, Dale to the right, and in between them, wearing handcuffs, was Jesse James.

They'd read him his rights and waited as the next set of arriving police used a pair of bolt-cutters to open the gate. Now they were walking the three blocks back to the station, getting a little one-on-one time with the man they'd been working so hard to hunt down. Percy had been working up something profound to say. Dale, however, always the straightforward type, beat him to it and just said, "Why?"

Jesse James laughed, a sneer across his sweaty face. They were all dripping sweat in the soupy New Orleans air.

"Why?" he repeated. "Why else? For the same reason that groups have fought this injustice for a hundred years. To cleanse our society. But I'm betting you think it's just me and maybe a few buddies. You'd be terribly mistaken. I'm part of something big."

"The KGC," Percy said.

Jesse James was visibly stunned, and for a moment, he

didn't reply. Then the sneer returned. "That's right. We're the Second Knights of the Golden Circle." He stopped walking. Percy and Dale stopped too. "And our aim is to do whatever it is we can to make this society decent for good, white folk again." He looked at Percy. "Highly addictive drugs. Laced pot. With a special ingredient. Get your people hooked, Agent Gordon, so we can kill off all the..." He said the N word, and he spat on Percy.

Percy had been called the N word four times now during his time as an agent. He'd always been able to stay detached. When a person said that word, they wanted a reaction. To remain unaffected would piss the person off a whole lot more than lashing out.

But being spat upon ... that was harder to stay calm about.

That had happened one other time. It had hit his jacket. This time, James' spit had hit his cheek, his neck. Percy saw Dale gritting his teeth on the other side of James. Percy counted down, calming his anger. *Four, three, two, one.* He wiped his cheek with his jacket and said, "You just assaulted a federal agent. Not too bright, are you, Jesse James?"

Dale grabbed James' shirt and pulled him in close. Percy reached a hand out to Dale and gave him a look that said, *Keep your cool.* "So that's *really* what this is all about?" Dale growled. "Just a bunch of murdering, racist scumbags? How the hell did you get involved in all this?"

Another ugly smile from Jesse James. Dripping sweat. A pinkish tinge to his skin. His eyes flicked between Percy and Dale. He was enjoying himself. "This is the point in our story where the heroes want to know where I come from. Why I've done this. A bit of understanding. Some backstory. Maybe I had a shitty childhood. Daddy wasn't there. Mommy didn't let me see black people, told me they were real bad. Maybe a black man hurt my sister. Maybe someone beat the shit out of me. Maybe someone touched me. But things aren't always that perfect or that complex. I am what I am. I'm a man who wants things the way they were, who wants the balance back. My name is Jesse Nathaniel Richter. I'm from Jackson, Mississippi. I'm twenty-seven years old. I have a finance degree from Louisiana State University, and I quit my job one year ago to become a Knight of the Golden Circle. I've brought more change to this region than anyone has in *years*. The people of this city know my name. The blacks whisper it in the dark. I'm their bogeyman. I'm their specter of death."

"Not anymore, you're not," Percy said. "The specter of death is in handcuffs."

"You think that matters?" He laughed a little, shaking his head. "I see now. You've been focused on me. Like I'm the head of this snake. I've done my part, and I'm proud. But this is so much bigger than me. And as soon as they've heard that you've brought me in, they'll roll out the Great Contingency."

Dale took a step closer to him. "If you're not in charge of this, who is? And what the hell is 'the Great Contingency?'"

The nasty sneer remained on James' face. "I won't sell out my brother knights, but I have no qualms about telling you the Great Contingency. I bet you thought this was your next great mystery to figure out. Let me save you the trouble. If this operation was ever to be compromised, *all* the drugs are going to hit the streets. At once. Every black community in New Orleans, Biloxi, Mobile, and Pensacola. We're going to flood this region. And it will be a glorious bloodshed." He lowered his face, eyes locked on Dale, smile broadening, teeth baring.

Percy and Dale exchanged a look. This had been in the back of Percy's mind the whole time—that whoever was behind the drug deaths was testing out their system, and ultimately they would find a way to get out as many drugs as possible. The longer he investigated the case with Dale, the more he began to realize that it wasn't about money. It was about death.

"Speaking of my brother knights..." James said. He put his front teeth over his lip, sucked in a big breath, leaned his head back, and belted out a whistle.

There were footsteps around them. Some from the the front. Some from behind. Some from the sides. Figures stepped out of the darkness. All white. All with guns. One had red hair, another brown, and the others were blond. Percy recognized the brunette. He wore a paisley shirt. He was the man he and Dale had chased earlier.

Percy's pulse quickened. He looked at Dale. Dale was concerned but confident, almost slightly thrilled. The threat of imminent death. That crazy son of a bitch.

"Did you really think I'd go out to that cemetery all by my lonesome?" James said. "Again, I think you're really underestimating the Knights of the Golden Circle."

The men closed in from all sides. They were only feet away. Handguns pointed at Percy and Dale, inconspicuously, casually, from their hips. Percy and Dale were circled.

"We're a block and a half from a New Orleans Police station," Percy said.

"That's right. Which is why we're all gonna go our separate ways. No harm no foul. Take a look at these boys' faces. Take a good look. We don't care. We're out in the open now. Because the Great Contingency is upon you. Now go ahead and put those hands up."

Percy and Dale put their hands in the air. Dale grimaced as he did so. He hated taking orders.

James stepped away, his hands still fastened behind his back. The other men began walking backwards, slowly leaving, guns still aimed toward Percy and Dale as they slipped away into the shadows. James joined them.

"We'll see you soon," James said. "Real soon."

CHAPTER TWENTY-SIX

IT WAS STILL early in the morning. Bright and sunny. Cool, still, but moist and humid.

Luanne watched through the window, the one over the desk in her bedroom. Vehicles were parking outside the pole barn in the back. Cars and pickup trucks. Lots of them. Men got out of them, went into the barn.

This was the first time something like this had happened during the day, and it was the first time it had happened when she was home. The other times were at night, and she wasn't supposed to have known about them. She and the boys were always told to leave so that Dylan could have a poker night with his buddies. He made it adamantly clear that he didn't want them around. When Dylan was adamant about something, she didn't argue. But she did always find it strange. Who were these buddies? Dylan didn't have friends that she knew of, only acquaintances. He had such a disdain for people—her family, the people on TV, the people he encountered in town. She just couldn't picture him laughing at a poker table with a bunch of guys, smoking cigars and drinking beer.

One night, she'd had to return to the trailer. Tyler had forgotten his favorite toy. She left the boys watching a movie at Maria's and came back for the toy. When she got to the trailer, she'd seen a dozen cars parked outside the barn and light coming from the cracks around the barn's big sliding doors. It would have frightened her had she not recognized one of the vehicles as her cousin's, Jesse Richter's. Jesse and Dylan had spent a lot of time together in the last year, so it made sense that his vehicle was there. But what didn't make sense was the fact that they were in the barn. Dylan had told her that the card game would take place in the trailer, and he'd said there would be "four or five guys." There were a dozen vehicles at least parked outside the barn. Before she'd gotten Tyler's toy, she looked across the yard, squinting to see what she could in the crack of the barn. There were people in there. They were dressed in metal. Like medieval knights. Feathers came out of the top of their helmets.

It was certainly bizarre, but she didn't give it much thought. She figured it was some strange hobby of her husband's. Medieval reenactment, perhaps. They did that sort of thing in Pensacola, though her husband wasn't a history buff that she knew of.

Today, though, the men entering the barn were dressed plainly.

There was a tugging at her pants. She looked down. It was Tyler. Both boys were behind her.

"Mommy, can I have some chocolate?"

"You know you can't," she said. "You want something sweet, you get an apple."

He pouted and walked off. Caleb stepped closer to her, put his head against her side. There was a look of concern on his face. She put her arm around his shoulder.

"What's going on out there, Momma?"

Luanne shook her head. "I don't know," she said. "But Momma's gonna find out."

CHAPTER TWENTY-SEVEN

DYLAN SHOVED him against the side of the pole barn, and the metal made a loud sound that shot up and down the wall. They were on the backside of the barn, and Dylan could hear car doors shutting, people talking as they went into his barn for the meeting. Jesse looked at him with shock and a bit of fear.

Dylan backhanded him, hard, against the side of his face. When Jesse turned back to Dylan, his eyes were raging as his hand went to his cheek. A drop of blood came from the corner of his mouth. It was demeaning to slap a man like that, and it made Dylan feel good. Really good. He'd wanted to do this to Jesse Richter for a long time.

"Now we gotta use the Great Contingency plan because of you and your stupidity," Dylan said. He shoved Jesse again, back into the wall. Another loud metallic bang.

"But I've done more," Jesse pleaded. "We can salvage this. I got us a connection. With the Grizzly. He runs the whole area surrounding the French Quarter."

"Ohhhhh. You hooked us up with a *black* drug lord. Congratulations. Don't you get it, you stupid hick? The Great

Contingency ends this. All this is over because of *you*." He grabbed Jesse by the shirt. "You think you got your position in the KGC because you did a good job? The only reason I gave you the power is because I'm married to your idiot cousin." He put his hand over Jesse's face, squeezed into his bones. "But you're out now. You got that? The Great Contingency will be the hallmark moment of the Second Knights of the Golden Circle. And the second Jesse James will not be a part of it. Whatever plans we develop afterward, however we decide to proceed, you won't be a part of that either. You're done, Jesse."

Jesse looked at him, his eyes wet. "I can do better."

"I told you, you're done." Dylan almost laughed. He gave Jesse's face a little slap. "You gonna cry? Are you gonna cry, Jesse Richter? Just like your little bitch cousin."

Another slap. Harder.

Jesse's eyes still burned, still glistened. He put up his fists.

"Oh, look out, now!" Dylan said. "You gonna use that kung fu of yours on me, Jesse?" He put up his own fists and assumed a dramatic, Bruce Lee-esque position. "Yeeeooowww! Weeeeyahhhh!"

He laughed at Jesse.

Then he reached his right hand into his pocket. With his other hand, he threw a punch at Jesse, going intentionally high. Jesse made one of his martial arts moves to avoid Dylan's blow, as Dylan knew he would. Dylan moved to the right and pulled his hand from his pocket.

Jesse's eyes went wide. His body lurched forward. He landed against Dylan's chest. Dylan felt Jesse's whole body lose its strength. The knife had entered him below the rib cage. Jesse's cheek was on Dylan's shoulder. He breathed deeply, rapidly.

"Even now I'm protecting you, Jesse," Dylan whispered into his ear. "No major organs." Dylan yanked his hand back, and the knife came out of Jesse's side. Jesse screamed out. "Now get yourself to a damn hospital and never step foot on my property again. You hear?"

Jesse stumbled away, his hands on his wound. His face was white, and he was hunched over. There was hurt in his eyes, and he looked at Dylan with a mix of bewilderment and angered confusion. He quivered with a wave of pain then turned and hobbled off, bent in half. A hunchback.

Dylan smiled.

He looked at the knife. It had been a trusty friend for some time. A four-inch switchblade with a cherry handle. The blade was covered in blood. Dylan was wearing a dark blue flannel shirt. That would hide it. He wiped Jesse's blood away.

———

Dylan stepped in front of the group. It was so odd seeing them in broad daylight. They wore street clothes not their armor. They were confused, looking around the room. They sat in folding chairs facing him.

Dylan spoke. "I told you all to leave that knight shit at home because this here's our last meeting. We're moving forward with the Great Contingency."

They were murmurs from the other men, concerned looks.

"And that means—"

Dylan stopped. He'd seen something. Movement in the gap of the door. And in that briefest of moments, he recognized who he'd seen. It was a woman.

It was Luanne.

He'd known it was a mistake to allow her to stay in the trailer during the meeting, but she'd been gone when he did the planning for the impromptu gathering, and he hadn't had a chance to tell her to leave. And now there she was, looking through the crack. Not that it really mattered. She was an idiot. No threat whatsoever. More important was the fact that she hadn't listened to him. Again. This pissed him off. Pissed him off bad. He would have to take care of this situation.

But then a thought came to him.

He remembered how his desk had looked disrupted, like someone had been going through his things.

Luanne?

Was she up to something? Was she trying to figure out what he was doing? Maybe she wasn't such an idiot after all ...

But as quickly as the thoughts had come to him, he pushed them away. He couldn't delay even for a moment. The meeting had to continue. "The Great Contingency. We're dumping everything. Tonight. All the cities. Every last one of you is out on the streets tonight, getting the shit out. And *do not* use our bags. Use anything you can find. Randomly. Whatever's available. Nothing with the symbols."

He looked out at the hillbillies and realized that if this was to be the last meeting, he needed to make it impactful. They were looking for leadership, after all, a sense of identity and purpose. If he was going to get the rest of the drugs out with the Great Contingency tonight—which he needed to do to keep the investors happy while he and Henderson worked on their side plan—he needed to get the most out of these idiots.

"Everything you've worked for has led up to this moment. This is a historic moment for the South. When I look out on you men, I see a proud bunch. It's time that we do our part to take back the country that God ordained to us. You're soldiers. You're heroes. You're knights. So tonight, make this a date that will long be remembered. *The Second Knights of the Golden Circle's biggest triumph.*"

He said the last words with conviction, smacking his

hands together. This brought a ruckus response from the knights. They cheered, whooped, slapped each other on the shoulders.

Propaganda. Works every time.

Morons.

CHAPTER TWENTY-EIGHT

"ALLIE, I STAND CORRECTED," Dale said. "This is ... amazing."

He sat at the table in the office at the NOPD station with Allie and Percy. At the desk behind them, turned away, was Ervin, who was reading a magazine. Dale had been pouring over the Knights of the Golden Circle materials. Whereas yesterday he'd only looked at a couple of the books Allie had shown him—which he had utterly rejected—he was now looking at photocopies of actual letters from the collection of Lincoln's correspondence with direct references to the KGC. He held one of the copies in his hand.

"The North was crawling with KGC!" Dale said. "Listen to this, from a letter to Lincoln about concerns in Philadelphia." He read from the letter. "*Allow me to suggest to your excellency the propriety of using a portion of the secret service money placed at your disposal to discover the parties connected with a secret society called the Knights of the Golden Circle. There are strong suspicions of their existence in this City.* This was in 1861. The first year of the war."

He looked up from the letter—slack-jawed, wide-eyed—at

Allie and Percy. Allie just shook her head with mild exasperation. He'd always had a tendency of not listening to her, and this time, she'd more than proven him wrong.

Dale rapidly flipped through the photocopies in front of him. "Look at all this!" He was so stunned by the amount of data before him that he could hardly form words. "I just ... it's incredible. Why has no one heard about this?" He grabbed another one of the photocopies, one he'd looked at a few minutes earlier. "This one is about my beloved Indiana, from a colonel in Indianapolis writing to Lincoln and Edwin Stanton, the Secretary of War. Dated 1863, right in the middle of the war. He says there were KGC lodges in every county in Indiana and that there were 92,000 suspected members in Indianapolis alone."

Allie gave him a wry look. "You always used to say that only great people came out of Indiana."

"Yeah, yeah, yeah," Dale said with a smile, not breaking his concentration from the letter. "The colonel talks about signs and oaths and handshakes. He said there were five-pointed copper stars that could be hidden under a coat and revealed to Confederate prisoners or, potentially, invaders to reveal that a person was a KGC supporter of the cause. And..." He poured over the letter, a treasure-trove of information. "It goes on and on and on. And this is just *one* of the letters! These are *primary sources*."

"Primary sources?" Percy said.

"Actual historic documents," Dale said. "Books and articles *about* history are secondary sources."

Dale put the photocopy down and eagerly reached for a book, one of the ones Allie had shown him the night before.

"That means these books you showed me yesterday might not be B.S. after all, Allie," he said.

"Oh really?" Allie said with dripping sarcasm, putting her

hand to her chest. "That is such a relief. Thank you, Mr. Historian."

Dale opened the book. "This claims to be the journal and diary of John Surratt, but I still have my doubts. It reads a little sensationally, and its editor is credited as the author of *Booth, The Assassin*." An important methodological component within the study of history was the ability to filter out the bias in one's sources.

"And who was John Surratt?" Percy said, looking even more confused.

Dale started to answer, but Allie cut in. "He was one of the conspirators during the Lincoln assassination," Allie said.

"'Conspirators'? Multiple?"

"There was an entire conspiracy surrounding the assassination," she said. "It wasn't just about killing Lincoln. They were going to kill the president, the secretary of state, and Vice President Johnson. Of course, Booth succeeded in killing Lincoln, but the man who tried to kill Seward, the secretary of state, was unsuccessful, and the guy who was going to kill Johnson chickened out. History remembers it as being a single assassination, but the intent was to fully decapitate the Union government."

Dale had been looking at the book while they were talking. "And if this text is to be believed, John Surratt was KGC. Listen to this description of the initiation ceremony. He goes into a mysterious building with a friend. They're stabbed with a blade by someone saying, 'Those who would pass here must face both fire and steel.' He's taken to a separate room; his friend is gone. He waits. Then he hears a voice, and the room is darkened. He's grabbed by 'gauntleted' hands, the clothes are torn off his chest, and he's blindfolded. He's pulled through a series of doors. More voices, questioning if he's to be trusted. Then he's pierced with a blade again, and he hears the same phrase as earlier, about passing through fire and steel. They make him kneel. One of his hands is on some-thing cold, the other is on a book. He's made to say an oath that he claims is 'terrible, horrible, and appalling.' Then the voices remind him that the penalty for breaking his oath is death. They scream this. *Death! Death!* His blindfold is torn off, and while he's blinded by light, he's pierced again with blades, all over his body. He sees a group of men around him in chain mail and helmets with red and white feathers. He discovers that his right hand had been resting on a Bible the whole time ... and under his other hand was the face of a corpse. When he looks farther back, he sees that he'd been kneeling on another corpse."

Dale closed the book.

"Pretty crazy stuff," he said. "And the text is really sensa-tional." He pointed at the editor's name. "I'm thinking this Dion Haco was a dime novelist."

"Maybe so," Allie said. "But there's no arguing with the primary sources. The KGC was real."

Percy leaned back in his seat, looking back toward the desk. "Erv, this is really fascinating stuff. Want to get your nose out of that magazine and learn something?"

Ervin turned the desk chair around. It squeaked. "Oh, yes. Why don't I come over there and help out the white folk too? Nah, I'm good. Thanks."

Percy smacked his hand on the table. "You know, son, why don't you go and wait in the lobby. There're other magazines out there. And a candy machine. More your speed."

"Whatever you say, Daddy."

Ervin stood up and rushed out of the office, slamming the door behind him.

There was thick tension in the room, and a normal person would have felt uncomfortable, but Dale was still fascinated by—and a lot more interested in—the new historical story before him. So he broke the ice by continuing. "According to some of the sources, everyone from Jesse James to John Wilkes Booth were KGC. And Albert Pike may very well have been KGC. He was the head of the Freemasons! Some of these symbols and rituals, they're very Mason-like themselves. The two had to be *connected*. It's all so fascinating. We have proof," he said poking his finger at the photocopy in front of him, "that the KGC was a significant factor in the Civil War. Why isn't this stuff in the history books?"

Dale saw Allie and Percy exchange a smile, like an inside joke. They were having a little fun at the expense of Dale's passion.

Allie patted him on the shoulder. "You can fix history when this assignment is over, Dale. For now, we need to figure out how this relates to the case. Back when Dad and I looked into KGC gold, we heard that the KGC had never ceased to exist, that it went further underground, that it was still out there, protecting the gold. But you said that Jesse James referred to his organization as the *Second* KGC?"

Dale and Percy nodded.

Percy was still looking toward the door, clearly concerned about Ervin. He pulled his attention back to the other two. "What about the symbols on the bags? Were you two able to crack the code last night?"

"Sort of," Allie said and pulled one of the books from the stack. She opened it up, flipped a few pages, and handed it to Percy. "I knew there was a code key in one of these books, but it took us a while to find it."

Dale stood up and looked over Percy's shoulder at the image in the book. It was a list of symbols—dots and lines and odd shapes—coordinated with the letters of the alphabet.

A	B	C	D	E	F	G	H	I	J	K	L	M	N
—	ꞁ	ꞁ	ˌ	╱	╲	╱	•	ᐧ	÷	•ꞁ	ꞁ•	•╱

O	P	Q	R	S	T	U	V	W	X	Y	Z	&	.
⟋	⅄	⟍	9	6	ᒪ	ᐧᒪ	ᒷ	⋁	⋀	S	ϕ	💲	=

The bags of drugs that had been collected were in the center of the table. Dale pointed at the bags. "The problem is, though, that the symbols on the drug bags are in the same style, but several of our symbols don't match up with the key."

Percy put the book down "Well, if they're the *Second* KGC, emulating the original, maybe they're emulating the original code as well."

Dale slowly nodded, not quite agreeing. He didn't want to think that their answer was unattainable. There had to be something there. "Maybe ... But..."

He stared at the symbols on the bags, looked back and forth between the bags and the key. And he noticed something that he hadn't picked up on last night. A consistency.

He was on to something ...

"Look at this," he said, picking up two of the bags. "All the codes on the tops of the bags are in the key. And..." He studied the symbols for a moment. "And every single one of our symbols that *don't* match the key are on the bottoms of the bags."

"Interesting..." Percy said.

Allie leaned in closer, her brow scrunched.

Dale stared at the bags. There had to be a connection. Why would all the new symbols be on the *bottoms* of the bags?

He looked for a similarity between the outlier symbols. They were so similar to the key, and yet—

Then he saw it. His answer. He had it.

"The bottom symbols. They're *upside down*," he said and looked at Percy and Allie. "Let's see what happens when we fold one of the bags in half."

Dale bent one of the bags in half, bringing the bottom symbols to the top. The clear plastic revealed both sets of markings. The symbols aligned with each other, filling in their gaps.

The symbols on top of the bag were:

And the symbols at the bottom of the bag were:

When they were combined, they formed:

Allie looked frantically between the bag and the code key in the book. "All the symbols are in the key," she said, bouncing in her seat. A moment later, though, her excitement abated. "But they spell T-H-I-R. *Thir* isn't a word."

"Just hold on," Dale said. "Let's figure out the others."

They folded all the other bags and decoded them. Allie wrote them down as they worked, and when they were done, they had a list.

TWEN, FOR, THIR, NULL

Percy rubbed his mustache. "Well, *for* and *null* are words, but what are T-W-E-N and T-H-I-R?"

The three of them were quiet for a moment as they stared at their list. There was the muffled sound of police work coming from behind the door.

Dale loved a good puzzle. It was all about connections. Connections between words, ideas, letters, numbers—

Numbers.

"Look!" Dale said, running his finger along the list. "Add T-Y to the end of all these words except *null*. What do you get?"

Allie smiled brightly. "*Twenty, thirty, forty.*"

"Exactly," Dale said. "Percentages. And look. *Null* was the bag that was given to Byron, the student at the high school. The personal bag that he smoked himself. Nothing happened to Byron. *Thirty* came from the bag Byron dealt to his friends. They felt the effects immediately but didn't start convulsing until a few minutes later in the classroom. The bag with *twenty* was the bag that Percy and I took off the dealer we chased down. The guy he had dealt to said he had taken the drugs before. He didn't die. He came back for more. And the *forty* bag we got from the Grizzly who said that the man who took the drugs started heaving almost immediately."

Percy nodded. "The higher the number, the higher the percentage of the poison."

"Exactly," Dale said. "The Second KGC were experimenting, seeing how much it took to kill someone. They wanted to get them hooked *then* kill them."

Dale shook a fist with satisfaction. He always loved cracking these sorts of mysteries in a case.

But quickly a realization struck him. Normally when he would make a breakthrough like this, it would mean a drastic shift of fortunes. He'd dash out the door to Arancia and zip away to catch the bad guy. But not this time. The Great Contingency was in swing.

Dale sat back down.

Allie leaned toward him. "Dale, what's wrong?"

"I figured it out too late. None of this matters now. They're dumping it all." Dale shook his head. "I was too late."

"Oh, Dale." She put her hands on his, which were resting on the table. Percy walked over, put another hand on Dale's shoulder.

People liked to joke about the concept of "feeling the love." But Dale could feel the love right then. He'd had a rare moment of despair, and now two people were there for him, touching him. It was nice to have.

Percy patted his shoulder. "Be right back. I'm gonna go check on Erv."

"Sure thing," Dale said.

Allie watched Percy leave then took her hands off Dale's.

"You really care. You're a good man," she said. "You were back then too. Don't think I didn't notice. But you could also be a world-class jerk. Now, though ... there's something different about you."

"I've changed. I was still becoming who I am now when we met. A few final growing pains. But we had a lot of good times."

"We did. A lot of bad times too. You were a real ass to me."

"Sometimes. But what about when you got your medical news. And you were scared. Who held you? Or when your cat got that little bump on her paw, and you freaked out. Who'd you call? Who talked you down?"

She chuckled. "It ended up being a spider bite that she had. I was sure worried, though." She paused, and the smile left her face. "Those are great times, but you're focusing only on the good."

Dale was so flabbergasted he could hardly respond. "Isn't that a *good* thing? To focus on the good instead of the bad."

She shook her head. "Bad is ten times more powerful than good. Like it or lump it. That's why the evening news is full of negativity. That's why a person can receive twenty compliments in a day but stay up that night thinking about the one nasty comment they got."

"I pity you, Allie. I really do. I choose to see the sunny side."

"Then why couldn't you say it? After all the times I told you I loved you."

"You know why. The number. You'd had seventeen boyfriends before me. *Seventeen.* You were only twenty-six years old. Not guys you dated. You said yourself that they were full-fledged boyfriends, dudes you cared about, wanted a future with."

"And you said I was 'fickle,'" she said, the victim once again.

"You'll forgive Number Eighteen for doubting that your feelings for him were genuine. And the fact that you kept dumping me—over and over—didn't particularly convince me either. Every time we hit a rough spot, you just left. That's fickle. You were my little runaway."

She rolled her eyes and tried to maintain her angered facade, but she grinned slightly. He'd used this joke on her before, and it amused her.

Dale continued. "You were my run-run-run-run-runaway." He was referencing the famous 1961 rock song by Del Shannon.

Allie was smiling now. "You can't always crack a joke to get out of difficult conversations, Dale. And I wasn't a runaway."

"That's right. You were more of a 'runaround Sue,'" Dale

said, expertly tossing in another Del Shannon reference. "Ya know, after you went out with that Greg guy."

Allie threw her hands up. But she was still smiling. "I wasn't a runaround either. I went on *one date* with Greg, and it was two months after you and I broke up, you crazy shit!" Still smiling, looking at him playfully. "And stop quoting Del Shannon."

"Would that make me '*Dale*' Shannon?" he said and arched an eyebrow, giving her a look of supremely self-assured cleverness.

Allie groaned. Loudly. "Nerd. You're nuttier than squirrel poo. You know, Dale, that big mouth of yours sure does get you in a lot of trouble." She smiled. "But it always pulls you right back out."

CHAPTER TWENTY-NINE

LUANNE TOOK another blow to the cheek, and she fell onto the bed, onto the blue-and-white blanket her mother had made. She was crying.

Dylan grabbed her shirt, pulled her back to her feet. "What were you doing at the barn, Luanne? What did you see?"

"I just wanted to see what was happening, why all those people were here at our home."

"I told you to stay in the trailer." He hit her again, this time with a closed fist. To her eye. Her head snapped back, and she felt blood rush to the skin. She stumbled back, nearly falling back onto the bed again.

His face was snarling, looking down upon her. His arms were taught, skin flush. "I saw what you did."

Luanne's sobs were so strong now, she could hardly reply. "I didn't do nothing. I just looked."

"The desk, Luanne. You've been rummaging around my desk."

She didn't reply, looked away from him. He'd found out.

She breathed even harder now. Her vision got lighter. She thought she might pass out.

"Come here," he said.

She slowly took a step toward him. Her head was bowed. She saw his shirt, smelled his sweat.

"Look up."

She craned her neck and looked up into his ugly eyes.

"Are you a detective now, Luanne? You've been real cute lately. Real cool. I had to give a lesson to your ignorant hillbilly cousin too, a little while ago. You and your stupid family have brought me nothing but a world of hurt. I want to know what exactly you think you're doing looking into my affairs."

Somehow, with the wounds she'd taken, being inches away from him and feeling his size, his power, her fear escaped her. If he'd already taken so much from her, what more could he take?

She set her jaw, determined. She narrowed her eyes and looked straight into him. "Who were those men in my barn?"

Dylan spoke through his teeth. "*Your* barn?"

"That's right. And why did you meet with Mick Henderson last night?"

Dylan looked at her for a couple moments and didn't say anything. For once, she had truly stunned him. She felt a rush of power. And pride. She continued to look into him and then made to step past him in a dismissive way, moving toward the front of the trailer. He shoved his arm in front of her, his hand smacking into the wall. It made a loud noise. She jumped. The trailer shook.

"No, no," he said.

He pulled his arm back to the side and swung it all the way across his body, catching the left side of her face. Her cheek exploded with pain, her body flew to the side, and she landed back on the bed.

Her face was in the blanket. Pain enveloped her. She felt his presence looming.

Dylan sniffed, cleared his throat. He slowly sat down next to her on the bed.

"We're not done here at all."

CHAPTER THIRTY

JESSE WAS DISGUSTED AT HIMSELF, having a black person driving him around—one wearing a gaudy, bright blue velvet suit with a matching fedora. But then he thought of the Grizzly as his chauffeur, his menial servant. This made him feel better about it.

They parked on Rampart Street outside the same police station the federal agents had tried to take Jesse to after the event in the cemetery. They were directly across the street from the rear side of the building. Both men looked over at a parking lot full of squad cars and personal vehicles.

"There it is," the Grizzly said. He was pointing at a bright orange sports car. "Where you find that car, you'll find them. That's the white guy's ride."

"Agent Conley," Jesse said.

The black guy, Agent Gordon, had said he worked for the DEA, but Conley was a mystery. He'd only said that he was part of the DOJ. That meant he could be FBI, OIG ... Hell, the DEA was part of the DOJ.

"How do you know this?" Jesse said. "My organization needs reputable intel."

He put a slight emphasis on the words *my organization.* The Grizzly needed to think that he was still part of the KGC.

"We've been tailing them," the Grizzly said. "You ever gonna tell me what this organization is?"

Jesse didn't appreciate the black man's tone, but he knew this was an opportunity. An opportunity to strike back at Dylan. "Why not? You've done us good. We're called the Knights of the Golden Circle. Our leader is Dylan Mercer in Pensacola. And I'll let you in on a little secret, Grizzly. Tonight we're releasing all the drugs. In all the cities. You mind your turf, and you'll be all right."

The Grizzly gave him a bizarre look. It was clear that he didn't understand why Jesse had unloaded all that information on him. It was almost a look of distrust. Jesse had laid it on too thick. In his excitement to exact some level of revenge against Dylan, he hadn't taken the time to carefully craft his persona, his projection of honesty. He'd been careless again.

But it didn't matter. Whether the Grizzly trusted him or not, he wouldn't let Jesse's bombshell piece of information about the Great Contingency go unheeded. He would let all his associates know. And this would put the damper on the KGC's last hurrah tonight.

Jesse was satisfied. He'd gotten his revenge on Dylan.

But he wasn't yet done with revenge. He still had to portion some out to the two men who had gotten him into this mess in the first place.

The federal agents.

He looked back to the orange car. It was an exotic of some sort, kind of like a Lamborghini. It was parked under a tree, diagonally across two spaces. Dale Conley must have been one hell of a douchebag.

It would be dangerous, yes, but Jesse was going to hover

around this police station. It was worth the risk. These two feds had been the catalyst that brought his life spiraling down.

Revenge was worth the risk.

CHAPTER THIRTY-ONE

LUANNE DIDN'T HESITATE as she handed Dylan's map over to the federal agent.

"It's my husband. Dylan," she said. "He's up to something. And I think it's connected to the drug deaths that have been in the news. All that stuff about symbols." She pointed at the small drawings on the map. "Dylan is searching for symbols."

Dale Conley pushed the sunglasses down his nose and studied the map.

He was not at all what she expected. She'd called the New Orleans Police Department and asked if someone on the drug task force would meet her midway so that she could get them critical information. When she announced herself as the same person who had telephoned them the list of locations, Special Agent Dale Conley of the DOJ was keen on speaking with her. With the words *federal agent* in her mind, she'd envisioned a middle-aged man in a suit with a big mustache and a gruff persona. But when a shiny orange car pulled up to the Biloxi police station—where she'd waited at a picnic table under a shade tree on the corner of the property—a man stepped out who looked nothing like the image in her head.

He wore a T-shirt and jeans and had a three-day beard. Sunglasses. He was in his thirties. Immensely handsome. Stepping out of the gleaming sports car, he looked like a movie star.

And he looked about as different from Dylan as one could possibly imagine.

She watched him study the map. "Sorry to make you drive to Biloxi. I just can't get too far from home. And I borrowed the car from a friend."

He waved it off, continued studying the map.

It was a bright day. Blue sky, big clouds. They stood under the shade tree next to the picnic table where she'd waited on him.

"These are the same cities you called in. Where he put the mark for Pensacola is pretty far north. More like the 'Pensacola area.' Cantonment, maybe Ensley," Conley said.

Luanne was impressed. He had a good command of the Pensacola region.

"Any idea what the drawings mean?" he said.

She shook her head. "No clue. But I'm sure they're connected to these strange meetings he's been having this past year. At our home. With a bunch of men. I don't know any of them except my cousin, Jesse Richter."

Conley looked up from the map when she said her cousin's name.

"And he had a meeting last night in Pensacola," she said, "with some rich-looking guys in suits. One of them was Mick Henderson."

"Who's that?"

"A land developer. He's a big deal in Pensacola. There're buildings in town named after the Henderson family."

Conley ran a hand along his chin. He gazed past her, thinking deeply. He turned his attention to the map in his hand. "A land developer..."

"I heard Dylan on the phone with Henderson last night. It sounded very urgent. He mentioned that he was going to a cemetery to find coordinates this morning. He said something about a great contingency, that it was going to happen tonight."

Conley looked up from the map. "*Tonight?*"

By the shocked look on Conley's face, Luanne realized that whatever Dylan was involved in was huge. No wonder he was dealing with Mick Henderson.

Conley looked around, frantically, like he was deciding whether he should stay or hightail it back to New Orleans. But when his gaze turned to her, the expression on his face suddenly changed. He studied her. A look of concern fell over him.

He'd seen the marks. She lowered her head, tried to hide.

"What happened?" he said.

"My husband is a ... difficult man."

He looked at her for a moment. There were the sounds of birds in the branches above them, cars on the street. Then he reached both of his hands toward her face. Slowly. He placed them lightly on her sunglasses. She did nothing to stop him. He had a gentle touch. He took the sunglasses off.

Conley's mouth opened. The look of concern washed away, replaced by one of shock and deep sadness.

She'd worn her largest pair of sunglasses. The lenses were big and round; the rims were gold. They looked cute on her. And they were big enough to hide what had happened to her eye.

She had tried putting makeup on it before she left. To no avail. A wide area of the skin surrounding her right eye was deep, dark indigo. Puffy, swollen, with a glossy shine. The eyelids on that side were nearly shut, just a sliver of her eye visible, which was bloodied, deep red surrounding the blue center.

The sunglasses had also evened her face out a bit. Now that they were off, Conley would be able to see that her right cheek was bigger than the other. Pinker. With scratch lines.

It was warm and humid, but she was wearing long sleeves that, along with her jeans, hid most everything else—except the finger marks on her neck that also couldn't be hidden with makeup.

"Oh my god," Conley said. "Your ... husband?"

She nodded. Her eyes watered.

He looked her over. His gaze fell to her long sleeves. "Where else did he hurt you?" His voice quivered with anger.

She didn't mean to, but her hands went toward the button of her jeans. Her eyes cast down that direction too.

Conley's mouth opened in shock again, and his face went white. He took a deep breath. Composed himself. "We have to get you to a hospital."

Nothing good would come from going to the hospital. It would delay her return, and when Dylan found out that she'd gone, his wrath would be terrible.

"I can't," she pleaded. "Please, I can't be gone long."

"Tell me about your husband, Mrs. Mercer. Who is Dylan?"

"Call me Luanne. Please."

"Okay," he said with a smile. A great smile. Straight, white teeth. "And call me Dale."

She smiled back.

"Okay, Dale," she said. The smile on her face vanished as soon as she started talking about her husband. "Dylan's from Indiana. He moved down here twelve years ago after he was fired by Eli Lilly pharmaceuticals. For gross negligence."

"What did he do at Lilly?"

"He was a chemist."

Dale's mouth went straight, his jaw set, as though he was suppressing anger. "Go on."

"He's been in an out of work since I've known him. For the last year he's been working in his field again. From home. Shipping pharmaceuticals. Though, I think he's lied to me about that the whole time."

"I would be inclined to agree," he said, still suppressing some sort of conflict within himself. It was clear that he was putting pieces together about her husband, connecting what she was saying with what he already knew, building up a case against Dylan.

"What kind of a man is Dylan?" Dale said. "Does he have a history with hate groups?"

Luanne shook her head. "He just hates everybody. He's one man against the world. He hates the people who fired him. Says it wasn't his fault. He hates Southerners. You know, now that I know he's involved in these drug deaths..." She paused for a moment, truly processing for the first time that her husband was responsible for countless deaths. "Now that I know that, I can tell you that whatever his reasoning, he's not doing it for a cause. He doesn't hate black people anymore than he hates everyone else."

The more she described Dylan's hatred, the more upset she became. By the end, her voice was shaking. These last couple days she was beginning to realize that Dylan wasn't just "grouchy" or "introverted" as she'd convinced herself all these years. He was dangerous. She was in danger. And so were her boys.

Dale put a comforting hand on her shoulder. She looked at him. He took off his sunglasses and gave her a reassuring look. It told her that everything was going to be okay. He was a kind man. His hand felt warm through her shirt. She put her own hand on top of it, rubbed her fingers over his knuckles.

She had been so impulsive lately, acting upon her desires,

no longer waiting for an approval from Dylan or anyone else. So she did something very impulsive just then.

She leaned up and kissed Dale.

His stubble tickled her lips. It was different than Dylan's sweaty beard. The whiskers were softer, more refined. He tasted better too. Higher quality. A better vintage. A better man. He reminded her of Alec Corber.

Though she'd savored it, the moment was over as soon it started. He'd immediately put his other hand on her shoulder and gently pushed her back. He must have thought she was being inappropriate.

When she opened her eyes, she saw that there was a strange expression in his eyes, and she knew immediately what it meant. It was more than just the fact she'd been inappropriate.

He had a girl.

Luanne felt guilty. She hadn't an ounce of guilt for kissing someone other than Dylan, but she felt ashamed that she'd put Dale in this position.

CHAPTER THIRTY-TWO

Dale was stunned.

How could Luanne Mercer have possibly thought her actions were appropriate? And why had she done it? It was both awkward and confusing.

Then he noticed again her massive black eye. The marks on her neck. And he saw a perplexed look in her eyes. Dale's experiences at the BEI had shown him that people often acted in highly unpredictable ways during times of extreme mental and physical stress.

There was something else in Dale's mind, some other objection to what had just happened.

Guilt.

He couldn't entirely understand his guilty sensation, but as soon as he pushed himself away from Luanne, he felt like telling Allie about what had happened, being truthful with her. Which meant only one thing. Something had resurfaced. Some level of feeling for Allie was there.

Oh, shit.

"I'm so sorry," Luanne said. "You have someone, don't you?"

Dale stammered. "I ... I don't ... Maybe."

"That was improper of me." She looked to the ground.

"Don't sweat it. There are bigger things for us to be concerned with. I need to examine this map, and you need to take care of yourself. I wish I could persuade you to visit a hospital."

She shook her head.

"Do you have children?" Dale said.

Her eyes went wide. "Do you think they're in any danger?"

Dale calculated his response. "I think you need to take them someplace safe for the next couple days. Until my team and I can get this figured out."

Luanne panicked, looking left and right. "Oh my god. How could I be so careless? What if something's happened to them since I left?"

Dale tried to say something—there were so many important questions he still needed to ask her—but she was already running to her car.

CHAPTER THIRTY-THREE

JESSE STOOD at the filling station across the street from the building he was monitoring—the NOPD District 1 Station. He'd been loitering for hours. In his hand was a soda he'd bought from the convenience store. He was using it as a prop, something to keep his hands busy, to look less like he was stalking.

The orange sports car had left a couple hours ago. But Jesse had a damn good reason for staying behind.

Both of the agents had left the station and approached the car. Jesse got in his truck, ready to follow them. But when Agent Conley got in the car, his partner stayed behind. Agent Gordon. The DEA agent. The black agent.

Jesse killed the engine then.

He was going to follow Gordon. It would be a lot sweeter to exact his revenge on the black one.

But it had been two hours since Gordon had gone back into the station, and Jesse was getting discouraged.

The station's back door—which led to the rear parking lot —swung open, and out stormed a black teenage boy with a large Afro. Moments later another person came out and followed him.

Percy Gordon.

Gordon chased after the boy. The boy didn't sprint away from him; he just kept on walking. This was no escape attempt. There was a different sense of urgency to their situation. The two of them knew each other.

Gordon put his hand on the boy's shoulder and turned him around. This pissed the boy off, and he brushed the hand aside. An argument followed. Jesse could hear their voices across the street but couldn't make out what they were saying. It was clear, though, that they were extremely angry at each other. He caught the occasional word. *Never. You. Not going to. Hate. Your decision.*

Yes, the two of them definitely knew each other. They knew each other quite well.

"So," Jesse said to himself with a smile, "Mr. DEA has a son."

———

Jesse parked his truck. After the argument had ended, the kid had taken off, leaving Gordon behind. Jesse had driven a couple blocks up to get ahead of him.

He stepped out of the truck and walked around the building, turned the corner. They were alone, he and the boy with the Afro, walking toward each other.

The kid had his hands in his pockets, looking at the ground, shuffling forward. When they were about twenty feet apart, Jesse called out to him. "How's it going?"

He chose his tone carefully. With a lot of his victims, he'd played the fool, the bumbling simpleton. But he had been able to tell when he watched the argument with Gordon that this kid had an attitude. Jesse would have to play it friendly ...

but cool. He didn't smile, not really, just gave his face a believable, authentic look.

When the kid looked up from the ground and saw Jesse, there was a reaction, something like a slight revulsion. Like he'd taken one look at Jesse's skin and knew he hated him.

The feeling is mutual.

"Man, piss off," the kid said.

"Looks like you're having a hard time. I got something that can help."

"Get the hell out of my way."

Jesse glanced left and right, dramatically, letting the kid know that what he was about to show him was private. And secretive. He reached into his pocket, inconspicuously, and partially revealed a bag of his pot. "You party?"

The kid's expression changed drastically. A slight smile.

Jesse gave him a knowing look. Transmitted his trustworthiness. Fooled him. Fooled yet another one of them.

But this one was special. This one was Percy Gordon's son.

CHAPTER THIRTY-FOUR

"THE GREAT CONTINGENCY is happening *tonight*, Allie," Dale said. "We have to figure out how these damn symbols connect to everything. Fast."

Dylan Mercer's map was on the table in the office at the New Orleans police station. It was a photocopy of the original that Dale had gotten from Luanne. Dale and Allie had scribbled some notes along the side. She was beside him. Both of them were standing at the table, leaned over the map.

It was crudely drawn. Almost childish. Somehow this made it even more perplexing. And creepy.

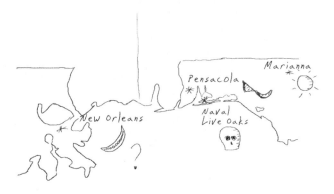

"Dad and I were just starting to look into the KGC gold when he passed. It wasn't long after you and I broke up."

"The last thing you two worked on?"

She nodded.

Dale thought back to the previous day when he'd dismissed the idea of KGC gold and those looking for it. He felt like an ass.

"Cancer had other plans for us," Allie said. She cleared her throat, refocused, pointed at the map. "See, each KGC symbol is supposed to point to another location. At each new location you either find the treasure or, more likely, another clue that takes you further along the search. There was supposed to be a system for coordinating the locations, but these four spots are more or less a straight east-west line along the coast. Doesn't make sense. Also, since the symbols are supposed to be in cemeteries and parks and places like that, I don't understand Naval Live Oaks. Didn't you say it's a nature preserve?"

"Yes, but there's a Civil War connection. The Confederates occupied the land in 1861, and the Civil War was also the effective end of the necessity for live oak timber with the development of ironclad ships. I looked into Marianna too. Another Civil War connection. A pretty huge one, as a matter of fact. Florida's governor during the Civil War, John Milton, was such an adamant supporter of the cause that he said death would be preferable to rejoining the Union. Shot himself in the head. He's buried in Marianna."

"Another cemetery," Allie said. Her eyes lit up in the way that they did when the pieces of a puzzle were coming together. "Of course all the KGC symbols would have ties to the Civil War."

She liked solving a riddle just as much as he did. He'd almost forgotten about moments like this, working on a puzzle together. It was something that he'd not experienced with any woman before. Or any woman since. The partnership. The cooperation.

Now they were working together again. Standing close. Their forearms brushed occasionally, and her smooth skin tickled his arm hair. He noticed her body heat, and when she would turn to say something to him, there was a moment of slight awkwardness, the kind of moment when you realize that you're too far into someone's personal space. But neither one of them retreated. She was wearing a T-shirt and jeans again, and like the shirt she wore yesterday, this one was a V-neck, a bit deeper, revealing more of her chest when she bent over. When he spoke to her, that close, in her personal space, he could see the detail in the freckles on her cheeks.

This time when she looked up, with that bit of historical excitement in her eyes, there was a slight moment when her expression changed. Her eyes lingered. Blue. The corners of her mouth dipped down. Not a frown. Something earnest. A recognition.

She smiled and turned away, back to the map. "But what about the symbols? Where could they be pointing?"

Dale looked at the symbols. They were scattered, seemingly random. What could it mean? What indeed? "I just don't know," he said. "Evidently Dylan's not entirely sure either since he has this question mark next to the New Orleans symbol."

Allie stood up straight. "Why didn't it work?"

"My guess is he had his doubts about the New Orleans symbol until last night when he heard from Jesse Richter. The creep must have found the symbol in the cemetery right before we caught him."

He looked away from the map to find her gazing right at him, seriously.

"That's not what I meant," she said. "Why didn't *we* work?"

Dale shook his head, shrugged. "You tell me. You kept throwing me away."

"That's right. I was 'fickle,' wasn't I? That's what you used to call me," she said, again finding a hurt to relive. She was that type of person: a hurt-collector. She held them close.

"Yes, you were fickle. I was your eighteenth boyfriend, after all. You threw away seventeen others before me."

"Dale, I did love you. You can choose to believe that or not. I thought you were an amazing man. Even with all your faults. But now … you're so much more."

"So what you're saying is that this second edition of Dale is even better?" He gave her a goofy smile. It made her laugh, tossing her head back. The pale skin of her neck stretched out before him. Her wild, red hair bounced.

When she looked back, her eyes met his with that intensity again, and she touched his arm. Her fingers were on his forearm. They remained there.

He looked down. Fingers, so small. Pale. Freckles. There was a slight movement in them, casual, almost imperceptible, as they messed with his forearm hairs, the same hairs that had brushed against her skin earlier.

Her other hand came to his shoulder.

Something was happening. Potentially dangerous. But still he put his hand on her hip. That curve. His hand rested there so perfectly.

She was standing closer to him now, and she leaned up to look him in the eyes. He could smell her. Her hair smelled a certain way, and it was right below him now, filling his nostrils.

Smell—the human sense most tied to emotion. The only sense that skips right over reason and logic and goes straight to the amygdala. The primitive brain. The emotional brain. Her smell was intoxicating.

She continued to look deep into him. "I didn't throw you away, Dale. We just met at the wrong time."

When he had been with Allie, the voice inside his head had worked at a fever pitch and around the clock. *This isn't real*, the voice had told him when she started planning international trips for the two of them after their second date. *No one falls in love that fast.* After only a few more dates, when pictures of him started appearing on the walls of her apartment and she gave him a key, the voice said, *Dale, no. What are you doing? This isn't genuine. It's fickle.* A couple months into the relationship, when he found out that he was her eighteenth adult boyfriend in her ninth year of adulthood, the voice said, *See? What more proof do you need? You're an amusement to her.* But Dale didn't listen. And a month later, when Allie even referred to herself as a "serial monogamist," Dale still pulled a Rod Stewart and tried to find a reason to believe that her feelings for him were legitimate. It was at this point that the voice in his head silenced, leaving him to his self-prescribed doom.

But now, as Dale stood with his hand on Allie's hip in their office at a New Orleans police station, the voice was back. And it was *screaming*. It warned him about what would happen. It reminded him of how he'd felt. The pain. The hollow loneliness. The rejection.

As he had in the past, though, Dale didn't listen to this voice coming from the rational side of his brain. Instead, he listened to the primitive brain. The smell. Her hair. Emotion. He looked at those blue eyes and felt that they knew now who he was. She recognized how he'd changed. There was something there. Caring. Love. She had really loved him back then too. And now life had thrust them back together.

Dale kissed her.

Taste and smell are interconnected. He'd smelled her hair. Now he tasted her lips, her soft tongue.

He put his other hand on her hips. Her curves. Her arms went to his shoulders. Their passion intensified, hands moving, exploring. Her fingers dug into his back.

This woman felt right. Up against him, in his arms. This was real.

They pulled apart. Panting. Looking at each other. But it wasn't a moment of reconsideration. Allie was as determined as he was. She went to the door, locked it, flipped off the lights. Dale started grabbing things from the table, carefully moving them to the boxes against the walls. In a movie, he would passionately shove the items to the floor and toss Allie upon the surface. But both of them respected history too much, and Allie joined him in carefully moving the delicate, old books. She kept her eyes on him as she did so. She was still short of breath, and there was an anxious, playful smile on her face.

The last item was removed. She rushed to him, their mouths, arms, bodies colliding.

And now Dale could toss her upon the table.

———

Little flashes. Small moments of time slipping away, escaping into history, gone forever.

His hands were upon her body. Her touch, so electric. The eyes, so much in them that he'd forgotten. Lines of light coming through the blinds, slicing the curves of her body. Subtle changes, differences from what he had known. Her hips. Her sides. This was real. Her eyes locked in on him. It was real. It really was. The movement. Rhythm. Her smile, a small laugh of joy just before she enjoyed herself the most, slipping into ecstasy. He'd wondered about that laugh when they were together. Had it meant that this was nothing but fun to her? More fickleness? No, this was real. She was simply happy. She was looking at him. Blue eyes. Telling him that she'd missed him. So much. So, so much.

———

Dale's eyes snapped open. He looked at the clock on the wall, just visible in the darkness. They'd been asleep for seven minutes. He'd set a mental alarm for ten minutes, but an idea about the case woke him early.

Allie was against him, naked, lying on his chest, her thigh draped over his legs, hand on his shoulder. Warm. Soft.

"Allie. Allie, wake up."

Allie blinked, squinting. Her wild hair was tussled.

Dale gently moved her then stood up and grabbed a clean photocopy of Dylan Mercer's map.

A visual had exploded in Dale's mind. He and Allie had been thinking of the four locations as a line down the coast. But what if they weren't in a line? What if they were a diamond? A long, stretched-out diamond.

The two middle locations—Pensacola and Naval Live Oaks—were so close together that you could almost consider them one dot on the map given the extreme distance between the western- and easternmost locations, New Orleans and Marianna. But in reality, Naval Live Oaks and the spot that Dylan Mercer had marked as "Pensacola" sat one on top of the other at a slanted angle. If these two locations were considered to be in north-south alignment, and New Orleans and Marianna were in east-west alignment ...

"X marks the spot, Allie! Look at this."

Dale grabbed a ruler from the desk and put it on the map. He drew a line from the Pensacola marker to the Naval Live Oaks marker then he drew another line between the markers for New Orleans and Marianna. He stabbed his finger at the point where the two lines intersected. It was right over downtown Pensacola.

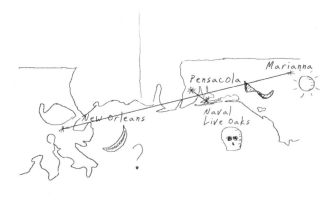

"Luanne Mercer said something about her husband going to a cemetery in Pensacola this morning, to find coordinates. There's a historic cemetery *smack dab in downtown Pensacola.* Right about there," he said, tapping his finger where the lines crossed. "It dates all the way back to the eighteenth century. That's where Mercer went. Luanne said he wasn't a true believer in his group's cause. Mercer must have used this drug operation as a front, having his minions find symbols for him. We put the pressure on him, and he had to dump all his drugs at once. That's why he was in such a hurry to find the coordinates this morning. Mercer's getting out while he can with his partner—a *land developer*. They're going to dig the gold up then take the money and run. He'll be going after the gold tonight after they dump the final drugs. If we don't catch him now ... we never will. Allie, I hate to say this, but put your clothes back on. We need to talk to Percy. And then we gotta get to Pensacola."

Allie sighed and reached for her bra, which was on the floor. "You sure do know how to make a girl feel special, Dale."

He grinned.

She paused before putting on her bra. "This was..."

Dale nodded. "Yeah. It was."

CHAPTER THIRTY-FIVE

DALE AND ALLIE pushed through the crowded main area of the police station, headed to the front door. They'd been told that Percy was outside.

"We'll take Arancia," Dale said. "I'll need your help in the cemetery, so when we—"

He was cut off by Detective Snyder, who stepped in front of him. He looked even more stressed than usual. "Agent Conley, we got word from one of the undercovers in Mobile. The drugs are starting to hit the streets."

It was happening. Dale had to hurry.

"Call Mobile. The mayor's office. They haven't been taking us seriously."

Snyder nodded and left.

Dale and Allie dashed to the front door.

———

Dale saw Percy sitting at a bench that faced the street. He was stooped over, elbows on his knees. Dale and Allie sprinted up to him.

"Percy," Dale said. "Did you hear?"

Percy nodded, didn't look up. He chewed his gum very slowly.

"Percy ... what's going on?"

He continued to look forward as he answered. "Erv. We had another argument. He ridiculed me for working with you. Called me a house ... N word. I don't care about that. But then he called the two of you crackers. I raised my hand to him. I told him he can call me whatever nasty name he wanted, but I wasn't going to let him insult two good people like you. And ... he took off, hasn't come back."

"Oh, Percy," Dale said. He was a little frustrated at Percy for letting a spat with his son interfere with his work at this critical juncture. "I'm sure he'll be fine. He's left before. He's a young man."

Percy shook his head. "This was delivered to the station."

He handed Dale a note.

I have your boy. Bourbon Street. Sundown. Jesse James

Allie read over Dale's shoulder. She looked at him.

Dale lowered the note. "Percy..."

He still hadn't looked up from the street. "I don't know why I raised my hand to him. I swatted his butt when he was a kid, but I'd never hit him." He looked up at Dale finally. His eyes were desperate. "You know that, right?"

"Of course, partner."

Percy looked back to the ground. "He told me that you don't raise a hand to a grown man. And he's right. I'm not letting him become a man. I'm holding on too tight."

Dale had seen more than his fair share of people crack under the intense pressure of the cases he investigated. He normally wouldn't have thought Percy would be the type.

But, then, he'd never had a partner whose child was abducted before.

Dale was in a tough fix. He had to hightail it to Pensacola if he was going to catch the man behind everything. But the rest of the drugs were being released, and his partner, the other person running the task force they'd spent weeks organizing, was a broken man. He needed to be extra diplomatic.

He knelt down. "Percy. Listen to me. I have to get to Pensacola. I have one shot to catch Jesse James' boss. Allie's coming with me. I need her expertise. You've got to help me out here. The drugs are already hitting the streets. I know it's tough, but until you meet Jesse James tonight, you have to do your damnedest running this task force. We need maximum police presence in all four cities. Someone has to coordinate all of it. Can you help me out?"

Percy slowly looked up. His eyes met Dale's. He straightened up, sat taller. His eyes focused, emotion giving way to purpose. His jaws moved as he started to chew his gum. And he nodded.

Percy was a professional. Dale knew he'd do what was right. He put a hand on Percy's shoulder and gave it a squeeze.

He then looked at Allie and flicked his eyes toward Arancia, parked in the rear lot under the shade of a tree, and the two of them ran toward her.

CHAPTER THIRTY-SIX

THE LIGHTS WERE OFF in the Grizzly's windowless office. The small television was on a wheeled cart, and it put out flickering light that cast long shadows from all the chess pieces. He sat at his desk, watching the program. He held a piece in his hand—a queen. He rolled it over his fingers slowly. It was from one of his favorite sets. It was carved from obsidian. For once, the Grizzly wasn't smiling. Rhino stood behind him.

The newscaster was finishing up her report. She'd told how the DEA agent's task force was scouring the streets in the targeted areas within New Orleans, Biloxi, Mobile, and Pensacola. They'd seized massive amounts of the drugs already, arrested several dealers. And there had been no new deaths.

Word had spread.

Another story began. Something lighter. A feel-good piece about a dog. The Grizzly reached out and turned down the volume.

"You figure the DEA will give you a medal?" Rhino joked.

The Grizzly still didn't smile. "It wasn't charity that made me tell the other drug lords what I learned from Jesse James. Purely business. And it's still early. People will die tonight, and some of that blood will be on my hands." He watched the silent TV for a moment, rolling the queen over his fingers. "I could have gone to the agents as soon as James contacted me. They'll figure that out." He paused again. "And they'll also figure out that I double-crossed them."

CHAPTER THIRTY-SEVEN

IT WAS a three-hour drive to Pensacola. Dale had Arancia's emergency light hanging from the rearview mirror, and the siren was blaring. The V8 roared. The traffic continued to heed way, and he pushed the speedometer well past the speed limit. This cut into the three hours, but still it was a long trip.

Allie ran her hand along the dash. "Oh, yes, Arancia," she said with a tone of remembrance. She'd spent plenty of time in that passenger seat. "Your orange, rare, Italian 'spy' car. Very inconspicuous." She rolled her eyes.

Dale chuckled.

He had been putting together the pieces of the case in his head, but part of him wanted to talk to Allie about what had happened, their time together in the station an hour earlier. It had been real. And Dale wasn't one to do those sort of things willy-nilly.

Sure, he had a well-deserved reputation as a ladies man, and his work as a federal agent had given people reason to label him as a James Bond type, the insinuation being that Dale had a life of similar promiscuity. But Dale didn't mess with the power of such actions. Certainly he went on lots of dates and was quite addicted to beautiful women—their company, their touch—but he respected the power that a full-on moment had. And he also respected the consequences. In real life, James Bond would be a petri dish of venereal disease, and he'd have kids spread out over the continents. Dale had zero desire for either kids or venereal disease.

The truth was, it had been a while.

And he was glad it was Allie.

But he had to put all of this on the back-burner of his mind and focus on the case. Luanne Mercer had stressed that her husband was urgent about his activities today. And if Dale didn't get to Pensacola soon, the moment to catch Mercer would be gone forever.

"Saint Michael's Cemetery. You're sure that's where he'll be?" Allie said.

"I'm certain that's the location, but Dylan Mercer won't be there. Luanne said he was getting the coordinates this morning. He'll be long gone. We need to search that cemetery to find the coordinates and track him down. His Second KGC is crumbling before his eyes. He'll need to get that gold and get out of town immediately. Hell, he'll probably try to skip the country."

Allie sighed and settled back into the seat. "It's always an adventure being with you, Dale."

She smiled at him.

By the way she said "being with you," Dale felt encouraged. It was validation of something he was feeling. Dale wasn't a normal person dreaming of a white picket fence, a Labrador, and 2.3 children. He had a difficult time even picturing himself as a husband. But he knew there was a future with Allie. He could figure it out. He enjoyed figuring things out as he went.

He smiled back.

She put her left hand on Arancia's shift knob, spread out her fingers. It was an invitation to hold her hand on the stick as they drove, like they had in the past.

Dale put his hand on hers.

CHAPTER THIRTY-EIGHT

LUANNE STEPPED through the office door and approached the counter. The smell of school was thick in the air. Sally, the elementary's plump, jolly secretary, sat behind the counter, partially hidden by a fern. She smiled at Luanne as she approached. But there was also a quizzical look in Sally's eyes.

"Help you, Luanne?"

Luanne put her arms on the counter. "I need to pull my boys out of class. Family emergency."

Again, the quizzical look. "Well ... Tyler's not here."

A shiver went over Luanne's skin. "Where is he?"

Sally paused. "Your husband picked him up. An hour ago." She took a binder from her desk and flipped a page. "For his dentist appointment."

Dark thoughts fell onto Luanne. Tyler had no appointment.

Sally's jovial smile turned to concern. "You still want me to get Caleb?"

"Yes," Luanne said. "And hurry."

CHAPTER THIRTY-NINE

THE POLICE STATION WAS CHAOTIC. Detective Snyder approached Percy.

"Okay, that's three cars we have south of Rampart," Snyder said. "I can get two more after six. And how many do you need to the east?"

Percy looked out into the madness surrounding him. Cops bustling everywhere, all hands tackling the Great Contingency. Fielding media calls, coordinating resources.

"As many as you can spare," Percy said.

Snyder nodded and quickly walked away.

What was the next step? He'd already coordinated with Biloxi. Mobile wasn't sure they had the resources. He would need to call them again and—

A thought intruded.

Erv.

With Jesse Richter. The man who had brought this chaos, the one who had hurt so many. Percy's heart ached. Literally. His chest felt tight, and cold ideas and images burned him from the inside out.

He thought about what Dale said, about how Percy needed to stay focused if he was going to be able to help Ervin and all the others. He needed to call Mobile. That's what he had to do.

Anything to distract himself for a few more minutes.

CHAPTER FORTY

It was 4:30 by the time Dale and Allie arrived at Saint Michael's Cemetery. Like Saint Louis Cemetery No. 2 that Dale had been to recently, it was old and sat near a raised highway, which put out a constant hum of traffic. But unlike Saint Louis, Saint Michael's graves were the traditional, in-ground type. It was a beautiful spot with stately tombs and monuments of varied heights and sizes. Majestic, ancient trees spread their wide branches out over the graves, and the occasional palm tree reminded you that you were in Florida.

But Dale didn't have time to be awed by the beauty. Instead his eyes focused on the sheer number of graves. It was far from the biggest cemetery he'd ever been to, but there were hundreds of graves before him. In fact, Dale didn't have to estimate the number. He'd found that out during his research.

Over 3,000.

"So many," Dale said as he put his hand over his eyes, shielding out the bright sun.

Allie's expression said she was thinking the same thing. "How the hell are we going to find it?"

"We'll find it," Dale said, hoping to sound more confident than he really was. "Everything works out if you give it time."

"That's exactly what we don't have: time."

They were on one of the roads that cut through the cemetery. Ahead of them and to the right was a small, brick building. An elderly woman exited the building and walked up to them, smiling. "Hi folks. Cemetery closes in thirty minutes. Just so you know."

Dale took out his badge. "Ma'am, we're looking for markings on a tomb, something that would give coordinates."

The old woman's eyes went wide. "I ... don't know of any coordinates. You're welcome to look."

Dale looked at the thousands of gravestones in front of him again.

"All right, Allie. Let's get started."

CHAPTER FORTY-ONE

"THANK YOU, MARIA," Luanne said and hung up the phone. She'd called everyone she could think of, driven to everywhere Dylan might have taken Tyler. No sign of them.

Her hands trembled. She looked down at Caleb, who was sitting at the table. He wore a look of concern. But he wasn't scared. He was determined. So brave for someone so young. He was her little man. He really was. He'd be a fine man someday.

She thought of her other boy, Tyler. Dylan had him. She didn't think that he would hurt the boy—he did love him, after all—but, then, she never thought that he could hurt her the way he had that morning. The last couple of days she'd realized that she didn't know her husband at all.

Or what he was capable of.

She thought of one more place to check, one more place Dylan might have taken her son.

"Come on," she said to Caleb. "We're going to make one more stop."

She walked out of the trailer into the bright sunlight

again. She held Caleb's hand. He hated when she did that. He thought he was too old for it. But he didn't complain today.

As she walked toward Maria's Dodge, a figure stepped out from behind the tree that grew beside the trailer.

Dylan.

She gasped, wrapped her arm around Caleb, shielding him.

"Hi Luanne."

She walked backwards, away from him, guiding Caleb with her arm. "Where's Tyler?"

"I got him someplace safe. Don't you worry about him." He looked at the Dodge and back to her. "Maria let you borrow her car. Nice of her. One of my boys says he saw you driving this morning. Followed you all the way to Pensacola till you got on the interstate. Said you were headed west. You were gone half the day. Go to the police, did you? Where'd you go, Luanne?"

"None of your damn business, Dylan."

He laughed. "Oh, she's got a little spine to her now." He ran his tongue over his teeth, turned his head and spat in the grass. "My map's gone. Tell me what you've been up to, bitch."

"No."

She felt movement behind her. Caleb jolted toward Dylan. She restrained him.

"You leave Momma alone!"

Dylan looked at him, scoffed. "Go inside, boy. Your momma and I are gonna have a nice, long chat."

A wave of panic rushed over Luanne. A sense of doom. Thoughts of that morning. The pain she still felt. His hands. The tearing of her clothes.

"Luanne," he said with a smile, "do I need to remind you that I have Tyler?"

Her thoughts went to her youngest child. And his safety.

This made her fear dissipate. She'd do whatever she had to for her boys.

She looked down.

"Go inside, Caleb."

"But, Momma..."

"Go."

Caleb hesitated then walked back to the trailer.

Dylan called out to him. "That's right. Listen to your mommy, pantywaist." His eyes returned to her. He had that look of glee again. "Let's take a ride, Luanne."

CHAPTER FORTY-TWO

IT WAS STARTING to get dark. They hadn't found any coordinates. They'd made several flimsy connections to symbols they discovered on some of the graves—desperate attempts at finding their answer—but Dale knew they weren't looking for more symbols. Coordinates, an address—whatever Dylan Mercer had found would be directions to the treasure he was hunting.

But it had been an hour, and while he was normally cool under pressure, the thousands of graves surrounding him were starting to give him a distinct feeling of desperation. Allie's body language, too, had changed. She looked defeated.

The old woman they'd met earlier walked up to them. "I can't wait any longer. I have to lock the gates. You need to leave."

Frustration came out of Dale. "Ma'am, please. This is official police business. Just go. We'll hop the fence when we're done."

The old woman thought this over. "All right. You're on your own."

———

It was dark. The temperature had dropped. The light from Dale's flashlight roamed the tombs.

Allie was beside him. "Dale, it's over. We'll never find it. Let's get you back to New Orleans so you can help Percy."

"It's here, Allie. I can't leave knowing it's here."

There was a burst of light in front of them. Dale grabbed Allie and pulled her behind a tree trunk.

It was a searchlight from a police car, probing the cemetery

"Dammit, someone spotted us," Dale said.

"Can't you just show your badge again? Explain why you're here?"

"No time."

Allie looked at him like he was crazy. And maybe he was being a bit nuts. But when Dale acted nuts, he got results.

He put his finger to his lips, shushing her. He shuffled them around to the other side of the tree as the light came near.

And then he saw it.

For a brief moment, the searchlight illuminated the backside of a tombstone, about ten feet away from them. At the bottom of the stone, near the ground, were two long sets of numbers.

Dale recognized the style of the numbers. Longitude and latitude.

Coordinates.

CHAPTER FORTY-THREE

PERCY CHECKED HIS WATCH AGAIN. 6:38. The note he received said "sundown." But it had been dark for almost an hour now.

He'd walked the main drag of Bourbon Street countless times already, the area with all the bars, all the shops. On TV, this stretch of Bourbon—the area you always see Mardi Gras footage from—seemed endless. But in reality, it was less than a mile. Another thing that had surprised Percy about the French Quarter was the fact that its party atmosphere wasn't relegated just to Mardi Gras. It was year-round. So, even though it wasn't yet seven o'clock, the crowd was thick—people shouting, bumping into each other. Drinks were flowing. Drunken zaniness.

And this is where Percy figured Jesse Richter wanted them to meet. Right in the middle of this madness, for the anonymity, for the safety of numbers. But he couldn't get over the fact that an hour had passed. Maybe Percy should have gone farther down Bourbon Street, past all the craziness. He cursed himself. His son's life was at risk, and he was being foolishly careless.

He turned around again to walk farther down the road, and then he saw him.

Jesse Richter stood dead center in Bourbon Street.

People funneled around him, laughing, stumbling. Richter's face was set. Just a small rise in the corner of his mouth. Beside him was Ervin. Richter's arm was behind Erv's back. Did he have a gun?

Percy felt himself move toward the pair. It had numbed his senses so much, seeing his child in danger, that it was as though his body was moving of its own accord. He ended up three feet away.

The evil from Jesse Richter's eyes bore right into Percy. From Ervin's eyes came fear. And a silent call for help.

"You started your Great Contingency, Richter," Percy said. "You got your drugs out. What do you want with my boy?"

Richter shook his head. "I don't want your boy. I want you. You brought my whole world crashing down. You and your fed buddy. The Great Contingency isn't my doing. They kicked me out. Because of you."

"No honor among racist killers, I suppose," Percy said. "But I guess they still like their revenge."

Jesse Richter smiled. "They do indeed."

He gave Ervin a little push toward Percy. Ervin stumbled forward a step or two. And then stepped back towards Richter.

"Don't do it, Dad!"

"I don't want you," Richter said. "I want your daddy, you dumb..."

He called his son the N word.

There was a flurry of motion as Ervin ignored the gun and threw several swings at Richter's face. It was a careless disregard for his own life brought on by a passionate, emotional response, but Percy was impressed. And proud. Ervin had shown some real bravery.

Percy sprang forward. The three men's limbs were entangled. There were blows. Screams from the crowd around. People ran out of the way, jumped over them.

Percy had a hold of Richter's ankle. Then he took a punch to the back of the head. He was thrown down. He landed on something. Ervin. He looked in his son's face. Erv's eyes were fire. Percy glanced up. To his right, people were screaming. The crowd parted. Richter ran through them.

And disappeared into the masses.

CHAPTER FORTY-FOUR

DYLAN DROVE the Corvair down the curves of Fort Pickens Road on Pensacola Beach. It had started to rain. The window was down, and raindrops hit his arm. He could hear the waves to his left. There were still a few other cars out, returning to the condos and hotels or making their way back to Pensacola proper.

In the seat next to him was Luanne. She'd been giving him a lot of lip lately, but now she sat there silently with that same stupid, obedient look on her face. She also looked truly frightened—not of him but of what would happen to Tyler. She had nothing to be concerned about, of course. She knew he loved the boy. But that's who Luanne was—a paranoid weakling.

She'd shown a bit of bravery lately, though, which was why he was bringing her with him. Given her recent actions, he didn't know what she was capable of, and he was certain that she'd gone to the police.

He passed the last of the hotels, and an opening in the dunes to his left revealed the ocean for a moment. The waves were violent in the wind and rain, but the moonlight was bright and clear.

"You always liked the beach, Luanne."

She didn't reply.

"You've been so curious lately. I'll oblige. The group you saw this morning—it's a group of local hillbillies. Your cousin is my right-hand man. The drug deaths—that's us. I convinced these derelicts that they were joining up with a new version of a secret society from the Civil War. I read a few old books, wrote down their symbols, their ceremonies. And these fools ate it up. I sent them out into a holy war, to kill off the black people they hate so much. I sent them out looking for the old symbols for me and my partner, connecting their group back to the real, historic KGC. Your cousin found the last symbol. Now my partner and I just need to use it."

"Mick Henderson."

"Mmm-hmm."

"How are you going to use the symbols?"

"Gold, Luanne. The KGC buried gold all over the country. Caches of gold to fund future endeavors. There are idiots out there who think the real KGC never ended, that it's carried on for the last hundred years, still guarding the gold. But the reality is there are millions of dollars sitting in the ground for anyone who can figure out how to find it. After we dig it up tonight, I'm leaving here."

He turned to Luanne with a look that he hoped would frighten her.

"And I'm taking Tyler with me."

———

They walked down the boardwalk, over the dunes and toward the crashing waves. The beach was bathed in moonlight from a blueish-black sky. The rain poured, drenching him. On either side of him were Mick Henderson's construction projects. The one to the right was a fenced-off area with a few bulldozers and other pieces of equipment. The site to the left was much further along. A tower. Ten stories high. Cement. No windows, doors, or color. It was a gray skeleton reaching into the sky. The moonlight glistened off it as the rainwater rolled in sheets down its walls.

He gave Luanne a shove to the back, toward the site to the right. He wasn't letting her out of his sight. Not until this was all over.

Dylan moved the wet hair out of his eyes.

There was orange plastic fencing around the site, the soft, flexible type. Luanne straddled it and crossed into the site. He followed, pushing the wet plastic down with his hand. The ground had been broken at the site, and Dylan was careful to watch his step. The sand beneath his feet was already quite loose, and it would be easy to fall into a pit. There were pallets full of cement bags, some columns already in place, all the equipment, and a big, steel trash receptacle in the far corner. But he didn't see Mick Henderson

"Henderson?" he yelled into the darkness.

He grabbed the back of Luanne's shirt, stopped her. Listened. Noise to his right. Someone walked out from behind a crane. It was Henderson. He held a black umbrella. Rain poured off it.

"This is it," Dylan said and moved toward him, pushing Luanne as he did. "This is the right site. This is where the coordinates pointed."

Henderson leaned his umbrella back, and his eyes went to Luanne. "Is this your wife?"

Dylan gave his response a moment's thought. "That's right. This is Luanne. I thought she should be part of this."

Henderson was slow in response, speculative. "And you're sure this is the right site?"

"I'm certain. We broke ground at all these other sites for no reason. All the other maps were dead ends. This was the only set of coordinates." Dylan was shaking with anticipation, and he was getting frustrated with Henderson's apparent hesitance. He pointed at a bulldozer. "Let's get started. Show me how to use this shit, and let's find it."

But Henderson just looked back at him from beneath his umbrella. A smile—small at first but expanding—came to his lips. There was something about that smile that Dylan didn't like. Suddenly, he feared for his safety.

Had he been double-crossed?

Dylan sensed the revolver he'd brought with him, holstered behind his back. He might just need it. "What's going on, Henderson?"

Henderson just continued to smile. He raised his free hand and snapped his fingers.

From among the equipment and stacks of material, hidden in the shadows, emerged several men, all bearing shotguns and rifles. They came from all directions and walked slowly through the rain toward Dylan and Henderson.

Henderson's gaze lingered on Dylan as the other men closed in.

"Dylan Mercer, meet the real KGC."

CHAPTER FORTY-FIVE

ARANCIA'S ENGINE bellowed as she tore down the road that cut through the center of the thin island that was home to Pensacola Beach. At the cemetery, Dale had checked one of the maps he'd brought from the office in New Orleans—a detailed map with longitude and latitude—and narrowed the latitude to the island. While he drove, Allie—also well-versed in cartography—worked on guesstimating the longitude as best she could.

It was raining. Hard. Not a storm. No lightning or thunder. Just a heavy, warm, windy rain. Arancia's wipers swung back and forth rapidly. Dale hated that she was getting rained on.

Allie glanced up from the map and looked through the windshield again as they drove past the last of the hotels. She narrowed her eyes, trying to peer through the rain and darkness. Farther down the road, Dale could see the partially-finished forms of future hotels and condos. Pensacola Beach was expanding to the west.

As Allie looked ahead, she shouted out, "There! That must be it. A park."

On the other side of the road was a small sign bearing a park's name. Dale agreed with Allie's thinking—the other symbols had been at cemeteries and parks. This was their best bet.

Dale yanked Arancia over into the park's small, gravel parking lot and came to a quick stop. He put his hand on the door handle, turned to Allie. "Stay here. Okay? You don't have a gun, and—"

"Okay."

Dale grinned. You didn't have to tell Allie twice. She was a very brave woman—having been on a lot of dangerous adventures with her father—but she also wasn't stupid.

Dale pointed at the driver's seat. "There's a knife under the seat. If something should happen."

Allie reached into her purse and brought out a large knife. She raised an eyebrow.

"Of course. How silly of me," Dale said.

He ran out the door. Rain soaked him immediately. Ugh. He hated the feeling of wet clothes.

There was a path in front of him that went up the dune, through the sea oats. The wind whipped rain into his face, and his boots sank into the sand. It was a very light sand, hard to walk in. He ran up to the crest of the dune, taking out his gun as he did. The park was in front of him, to the right. A few tables and fire pits. A stretch of sand beyond and huge, thunderous waves.

Dale had finally made it to the beach.

He walked over to the tables and saw nothing, no one. And there was nowhere to hide. If this was Dylan Mercer's destination, he'd already visited.

Shit.

Dale lowered his gun and looked about, searching for a hole, a pile of sand, anything indicating that something had been dug up. And as he looked, he saw motion. Farther down the beach.

He cupped his hand over his eyes, shielding out the rain. The moonlight was bright and lit the beach ahead of him. About half a mile down the beach there was a tall tower, partially built, and beyond that another construction site in its early stages. And he saw people. A dozen or so. He could just make out their figures.

And their guns.

Dale sprinted back up the path. He threw Arancia's door open and dropped into the driver's seat, cringing as he realized that he was getting rain water all over the leather seat and sand in the carpeting.

"They're down the beach," he said to Allie.

He turned the key, and Arancia thundered back to life. He threw the stick into reverse, let off the clutch and gave her some gas. She roared. But she didn't move. Her tires spun.

He'd gotten her stuck in the sand.

Of all the bonehead, novice things he could do, he'd gotten Arancia stuck in the damn sand. He'd parked too far to side of the parking lot, where the gravel was sparse. He thought about how this would play out after the excitement of the mission, a tow truck having to put a big metal hook on her, someone else getting in the driver's seat. Dale's soul shuddered. He refocused on the mission, looked at Allie.

"I gotta run for it. I'll be back."

Allie nodded. "Go. Be safe." She looked at him earnestly as she said it.

He paused, just for moment, then he leaned over and kissed her.

He jumped back out of the car, shut the door. The road was to his right, but he had seen that it curved away from the beach prior to where the construction began. It would be quicker for him to reach the people he'd seen if he approached from the beach.

He ran back up the path, his boots sinking into the sand again. They were going to weigh him down. He dropped to the sand. It was cool and wet, soaking through the seat of his jeans. The rain poured on him. He fumbled with his wet laces and tore off his boots then his socks, tossed them in a pile, stood up, rolled up the cuffs of his 501s, and darted towards the surf, where the water would have packed the sand, making it easier to run on.

Rain pelted his face, his chest. He brushed the hair from his cheeks and eyes. His legs burned, heavy and cumbersome in the sand, as he made it his way to the waves. Then he hit the wet, packed sand of the surf, felt cool water between his toes, and took a right, sprinting along the crashing waves toward the people in the distance.

CHAPTER FORTY-SIX

LUANNE SHIVERED in the rain as it washed over the fresh wounds on her body. But still, there was a bit of happiness in her. Dylan had been thwarted. When the men had revealed themselves from their hiding, the look of shock on Dylan's face was thrilling to her. It had been a look of bewilderment and disgust as he viewed the men who had encircled them. Because they were just the type of people Dylan hated. Good old boys. Paunchy. Jowly. Some of them in tank tops. A couple with cowboy hats. Southerners. And while Luanne knew that the men were part of a group with racist motives, the fact that they were Southerners like her, people that Dylan truly despised, made her pleased that they were the ones who had ruined his plan.

Mick Henderson continued to give her husband a look of superiority. "We'd like to thank you, Mercer. We've been searching for this site for some time now. It had been lost to history. Couldn't have found it without the help of you and your boys."

Dylan stammered. It was one of the few times Luanne

had ever seen him at a loss for words. "But ... You can't do this. We had a deal."

"I can't?" He waved his hand, indicating all the armed men who surrounded them. "Your part in all this is over, Dylan Mercer. Leave. And remember," he said, the smile leaving his face, "we're watching you."

Dylan stammered again, trying to find something to say. Nothing came out. He looked at Luanne and then back to Henderson. He exhaled. And then he grabbed her wrist, turned around, and led them back over the fence and out of the construction site.

There was something moving. Out on the sand. At first, it looked like a random person walking the beach ... in the rain, for some reason. But the person wasn't walking. They were running. At a full sprint. A man. In jeans. And a white T-shirt. The moonlight lit him up clearly. There was a flash of light from his hand. A gun. She saw the face.

It was Dale.

Luanne smiled. With all the hell that was going on, with the uncertainty about Tyler, with the discovery that her husband was a killer, there was still no stopping the smile.

Because there was Dale.

Running with everything he had.

She had seen tonight the lowest a man could be. But now, almost as if God wanted to show her the difference, she saw the best a man could be. A hero.

Dylan had seen him too. He squinted, leaned forward. "What the hell?"

He turned to Luanne. Then his eyes lit up with that fury that he got when he was disrespected. He'd seen her smile. She couldn't help it.

"Who is that man, Luanne?"

She didn't answer him. She wasn't going to. She just continued to smile.

"He's a goddamn cop! Isn't he, Luanne?"

She said nothing.

He slapped her.

"Who is that asshole?" He grabbed her shoulders and shook her. "Why are you smiling like that? Did you screw him? Did you screw that cop, you little hillbilly, black-loving, Southern whore?"

She stepped into him, got on her tiptoes, as close to his face as she could. She spoke clearly and loudly. "No, Dylan. I didn't 'screw' him. I kissed him. Oh, yes, I disrespected you like that. I had myself all up against him. And it was good, Dylan. So good."

He raised his hand.

She didn't blink.

That look came to his face again, the confused look, the same look he had when he was stammering with Mick Henderson. He lowered his hand and looked her up and down.

Then he turned back toward the beach. Dale was closer now.

Dylan reached behind his back and took out his gun.

CHAPTER FORTY-SEVEN

JESSE PUSHED his way through the people. They were all staring at him with fright. There were screams. They darted away. He liked that. As panicked as he was, knowing that he was a hunted beast, he liked frightening the degenerates.

He had made a beeline to the nearest store. It was a shop. Full of junk. The walls were lined with Mardi Gras beads. Brightly-colored. Some with obnoxious shapes formed into the plastic. Marijuana leaves. Penises. It was all filthy, just like the people around him.

He shoved one of them out of his way. A woman. She fell over. He was looking for access to the second floor. All these buildings in the French Quarter had those famous balconies. They were apartments, surely. There had to be a way up there.

Then he saw it. A door in the back.

He approached it. More people cleared out of his way. The person working behind the counter—a gangly woman with dark hair, too many wrinkles—approached him. "You can't go back there."

He grabbed her by the face, extended a knee, and flipped

her entire body back behind the counter. People in the store screamed. He turned the doorknob. Wouldn't budge. He kicked the door, hard. Once. Twice. The wood around the handle cracked. A third kick, and the door flew open, smacked into the wall.

Stairs in front of him. He ran up them. It was dark, and on the second floor there was a hallway with apartment doors. A musty smell. Marijuana smoke. One of the doors was open, people pouring out of it. A party.

He moved into the crowd, through the apartment's doorway. There was hippie regalia on the walls. Tie-dye. Indian bullshit. Ahead, through the crowd and the clouds of pot, he could see open windows.

The balcony.

He stepped outside. A couple of the people on the balcony looked at him curiously, but most of them didn't notice. They were baked out of their minds, and it was likely an open party. They were dressed bizarrely. One man was shirtless. Another wore a tutu. All draped with plastic beads.

This is why he'd come, why he'd wanted to find a balcony. These people. These wretches. He looked down to Bourbon Street below. So many more of them. The place was crawling with them. And so many blacks. He wanted them gone. He wanted them all gone.

Below, to the left, he saw Agent Gordon and his son. They hadn't spotted him. Gordon was looking through the crowd, frantically.

Jesse scanned through the roaming, belching mass below him.

The last stand of Jesse James. And he was going to take as many of these shits out with him as he could.

He pulled out his gun. Wrapped his finger around the trigger.

And something grabbed him.

One of the degenerates. The shirtless one. He reeked of alcohol.

This was Jesse's last stand, and this goddamn freak wasn't going to stop him.

CHAPTER FORTY-EIGHT

DALE WAS sprinting so fast and so hard he thought he might pass out. His lungs burned like fire. The rain was soaking him, tearing into his face.

He traced the curves of the surf as he went. From running on the beach in the past, he knew there was an area near the waves where the wet sand packed down most tightly and made the best surface for running. You had to follow where the waves had receded—not all the way up to farthest point they'd reached but not too close to the water either, where the sand would get soppy. You had to find the sweet spot.

Right in front of him, a wave suddenly ran up farther on the beach than the others, and he splashed into the water. He stumbled forward a few paces, nearly recovered, then tumbled into the sand. It stuck to his T-shirt, and some got in his lips. He spat, pushed his hands down, and shoved himself up.

Back on his feet. Back to running. Sprinting. To stop Dylan Mercer. And help Luanne.

He had seen her. She was being pulled away from the

construction site, away from the group of people, by a tall man who had to be Dylan Mercer.

Dale thought again about the wounds Dylan had given her. He thought about the implication her body language had given as to what else Dylan had done. He thought about the ring he saw on Luanne's hand, the power of a symbol like that.

Dale spent a lot of his time chasing symbols—archaic and often anchored to myth. But that piece of metal around Luanne's finger meant something real. And Dylan had struck that. He had hurt that. There were men like him who were given the greatest gift a woman could offer. Her love. And they spat upon it. And then there were other guys who would never get that, who would look into the eyes of the woman they cared for, ask her if she ever wanted to see him again, and hear "No." And they'd walk out of her apartment, into the rain, to their car sitting under a streetlight, waiting to take them home.

He thought about Allie now. His second chance. The thoughts he'd had, the ideas. The image of Dale Conley in commitment to a woman. And his acceptance of these ideas. He would make this work. He'd accept Allie's love.

In the office. Her body. Her face. Her lips.

He thought of Luanne's lips. His kiss with her. There had been a wound so close to her lips. Love she'd given to a man had been thrown back at her, turned from poetry to poison. Smashed into her face. Bruises. Cuts.

His legs pushed harder, faster. He was going to get that monster away from her.

There was a *crack*. Loud but muffled by distance. A gunshot. Then another. And another. A *plop* to his left. A round had hit the water. A hiss and a *thwack* on the opposite side. Sand peppered his bare ankle, burned his skin. The shots were landing close. Dale hit the deck. Back into the sand again. He got as low as possible. Another shot. Another.

Dale counted them. Six. The shots stopped. He waited a moment. Nothing more. Six shots. Dylan Mercer had a revolver. And he'd emptied it.

Dale got back up. He saw Luanne and Dylan moving quickly now. Dylan had foolishly, passionately wasted his ammunition, and he knew that Dale wasn't going to give up. They were going to the tall, half-finished building. Dylan Mercer was going to hide.

Bullies were like that. They were cowards.

That just made Dale want to catch the guy even more.

CHAPTER FORTY-NINE

THE BUILDING WAS DAMP, and the wind whipping in through the open doorways and windows blew against Dylan's wet skin and soaked clothing. Cold. But at least he was out of the rain. He grasped Luanne's wrist tightly, pulled her up a stairwell. It was empty, unfinished, no handrail. Their footsteps echoed.

Onto the second floor. He rushed them to one of the windows. A gust of wind blew in his face. He looked down at the beach. No sign of the guy. He held a finger up to his lips and looked at Luanne. *Shut up*. Crashing waves. And whistling wind. He listened carefully.

Footsteps.

Slowing from a run. Approaching the building. Coming off the sand and into the gravel. Crunching. Getting closer.

"Up here!" Luanne screamed. She had her free hand cupped over her mouth.

The footsteps below hurried again, came to a run. They entered the stairwell.

"That's the last time you're gonna screw this up for me, Luanne." He clenched his hand into a fist and punched her hard. Her head flew back, wet hair snapping behind her, and she collapsed into a pile on the cement.

He faced the open doorway of the stairwell. The foot-steps grew louder. And then there he was.

He was dressed like Dylan. Jeans, a T-shirt. Dripping wet. He was barefoot. His shirt clung to his heaving chest. He held a gun. His mouth was open, taking in huge gulps of breath. His brown hair was plastered to his head. The man's eyes looked at Dylan for only a moment, measuring him, then they went to Luanne and quickly back to him, now filled with hate, rage.

Good. Dylan welcomed it.

The man started toward him. Palpable anger coursed through his arms which seemed taut with shaking restraint as they kept his gun leveled at Dylan. It was a little, pussy gun. Either a Detective Special or a Model 36.

"Who are you?" Dylan said.

It took the man a moment to respond, as though his anger was clouding his basic motor skills. "Special Agent Dale Conley."

"Dylan Mercer." He pointed to Luanne. "Did you touch my wife, Special Agent Dale Conley?"

Conley was about thirty feet away. Still approaching. Still aiming his gun. Dylan could see his features clearly now as he stepped into a patch of the bright moon light coming in through one of the open windows. His face was covered in a couple days' worth of beard. He was handsome in the way that guys in magazines modeling slacks and underwear were. No wonder Luanne had kissed the man. She was into all that cool crap.

Conley never answered his question. He just kept moving forward. The closer he got, the more Dylan could see the rage in his eyes, the hate. Conley hated the fact that Luanne was unconscious on the floor behind him, and he *really* hated the person who had done it. He hated Dylan.

When they were about ten feet apart, Conley stopped. He had been looking Dylan straight in the eye, never breaking his stare. Some sort of test of wills. The fool.

There was the sound of the waves beyond. Wind howled through the empty building. A lonely seagull squawked as it fought its way through the chaos back to wherever it called home, wherever its flock was.

Dylan looked at Conley's gun. With the rage that was in his eyes, Dylan knew Conley might kill him. "I shot at you as you were running up. Six times. I'm out of ammo."

Conley nodded. *I know.*

"Shooting an unarmed man, then?"

"Let me see your weapon."

Dylan slowly reached behind his back and took out his gun.

"Out the window," Conley said, motioning with his head, not breaking his stare.

Conley wasn't one to take any chances. Dylan tossed the gun out the window. It was so noisy with the wind and the waves, he didn't hear it land.

"Now what?"

Conley slowly reached behind his back, like Dylan had. His hand returned with a holster, and he put the little gun inside. He held it out before Dylan as if to display it to him. Then he bent over and put it on the ground, stood back up, and brushed it across the room with his foot. Dylan heard the leather of the holster slide across the cement to the wall several feet away.

Then Conley put up his fists, staggered his feet, lowered his weight into his hips.

"Oh, *mano a mano*, huh? Very admirable," Dylan said. He raised his fists. "You got it."

CHAPTER FIFTY

PERCY HEARD SCREAMS. People were looking up, pointing. On the second-floor balcony of the building in front of him, there was a struggle. And though Percy didn't see him at first, he knew it was Jesse Richter.

Two men were grappling. One was shirtless, sweaty, and draped in a massive amount of Mardi Gras beads. The man's back was turned, and Percy saw only brief glimpses of the other man. Then he pulled to the side, and Percy saw Jesse Richter.

Richter's face grimaced. Teeth bared, eyebrows in a V. He used one arm to fight off the shirtless man, and with the other he held a gun that was pointing down toward Bourbon Street. Richter kept looking at the gun, as though aiming down into the crowd below, but each time he did, the shirtless man reached for it again.

Richter was going to fire into the crowd.

But some random reveler was trying to stop him. The man was a goddamn hero. A half-naked hero covered in plastic beads.

Ervin spoke. "Dad..."

Hearing his son's voice solidified the urgency of the situation. Jesse Richter had gone kamikaze. He knew his time was up, and he was going to take out as many people as he could on his way out.

Percy drew his Colt and aimed it toward the balcony. He yelled out to Ervin without turning around.

"Get out of here, Erv. Go!"

Percy had only fired his weapon once in the line of service, a warning shot. But he knew he was going to have to do something a lot more serious now—if the shirtless hero would just move for a moment.

Percy only got little flashes of Jesse Richter. Most of what he saw was the other man's sweaty back and arms, his brightly-colored beads. They fought and fought. The hero was strong—or, at least, fighting with alcohol-fueled power.

Jesse Richter broke free for a moment and fired his gun once, twice, in rapid succession. The crowd on Bourbon Street erupted into chaos. To this point, many of them hadn't noticed the struggle as anything other than drunken zaniness. Now they knew. People ran, screamed. Percy scanned the area where the shots had gone. No bodies. No one injured.

A police siren sounded a few blocks away.

The two men continued to grapple. More of the man's back. If the hero would just get out of the way ...

Percy darted to the left, tried to get a better angle. People ran all around him, bumping into him, not noticing in their panic that he, too, had a gun.

Richter got a hand onto the face of the shirtless man and gave him a shove.

There was space between the two men. Richter was fully visible for just a moment. His whole torso.

Percy couldn't hesitate.

He fired. Three times. The sounds *cracked* off the buildings.

Jesse Richter moved left then right, almost an awkward dance, jolting as the three rounds entered his chest. The gun fell from his hand. He went toward the railing of the balcony, teetered for just a moment, then flipped over the edge, his body somersaulting forward as it fell through the air. Richter hit Bourbon Street with a wet thud. More screams. Richter's face was angled toward Percy. The body was about fifty feet away. Even dead, those eyes of his were malevolent.

Percy holstered his gun and whipped around. People were still running about, but some began to filter out of the shops and bars to see what had happened.

But none of them were his son.

"Ervin!"

The police siren wailed. Blue and red lights bounced off the walls, mixing with the brightly-colored lights of the bars and shops. People moved all around him. A uniformed cop came up to him. Asked him something. Urgently. Percy looked past him.

And then he saw Ervin, coming out of the shop behind him. Percy pushed past the cop, grabbed his son, and pulled him in tight.

CHAPTER FIFTY-ONE

As THE TWO men circled each other, Dale watched Dylan Mercer's face sliding in and out of the moonlight. A vague smile. Mercer was enjoying himself. Confident, as though he truly believed he was going to win.

Cute. Someone who actually thought his will was stronger than Dale's.

Still, Mercer was formidable. Well over six feet tall. All legs and arms. Large, square fists. His chest was thin but broad. Wide shoulders.

He was a rough-looking man. Kind of creepy. His hair was long and scraggly, with a few grays. His beard, too, was unruly, untrimmed. Within the beard, his mustache was longer, full-grown, as though it was his intent to wear a mustache, but he rarely shaved around it. It was all hidden in the wild, oily scruff.

Most striking was his demeanor. There were people who you could just read, and from Dylan Mercer, Dale saw nothing but spiritual decay. He thought back to when he and Percy had captured Jesse Richter, looking into the man's eyes and seeing his hatred, which had been based on a perverse ideology. Mercer, though, had no ideology.

He was nothing but unbridled hate. He was the kind of man who hated everyone but himself, someone with a chip on his shoulder carved out by the entire damn world. The ultimate in victim mentality. He hadn't done all this because he hated black people. He hated indiscriminately.

Dale really didn't like that the man hailed from Indiana. Since leaving the Hoosier State at the age of ten, Dale had built up a disproportionately glowing image of the place and its people. This assignment, more than anything, had brought that image crashing down. He'd discovered that Indiana had been infiltrated with the original KGC, and the Second KGC had started at the hands of a Hoosier. It was like finding out your childhood hero was a criminal.

Dale threw a jab, testing the waters. Mercer dodged it. There was that look of enjoyment on his face still. He threw his own punch, missing Dale by several inches. A light punch. He was experimenting too.

Dale glanced at Luanne. She breathed lightly. Her legs were folded against her, one arm resting beside her head. When Dale looked back at Dylan, he felt a fury. The man in front of him had done that to her.

Dale bolted forward with two swings, a left that missed and a right that connected.

He thought about what Allie had said, about negativity being ten times stronger than positivity. If she were right about that, it meant that Dale wouldn't be able to beat Mercer. It meant that hate would win. When they broke up, Dale had contended that the strength of their connection was the most important thing, that they could get over their differences. But Allie had said that the idea of *love conquers all* wasn't realistic. She said there were things in a relationship more important than love; it was her theory of negativity being tens time more potent taken to the ultimate level. She confused Dale. What could be more important than love?

Mercer wasn't going to win. Positivity and love were more powerful, not ten times weaker. Allie was wrong about that.

Wrong, wrong, wrong.

Dale threw a big roundhouse and cracked it across Mercer's jaw. The impact against Dale's knuckles was both painful and exhilarating. He wanted to punch the hate right out of the man.

Mercer staggered. The blow had been a good one, and it stunned him.

Dale hit him again, this punch to the opposite side of the face. Blood flung from his mouth. An uppercut to Mercer's ribs. He buckled.

Mercer swung back. His punch was unsteady and misplaced. Dale easily dodged it and threw another blow into Mercer's temple. Then his collarbone. His stomach.

Dale punched again and again and again. He punched the monster for every woman who felt the hands of her love bring pain to her flesh. He punched him for every child who quaked at the sight of his parents. He punched him for every quivering, cowering animal, shaking at the feet of some twisted, piece of shit person.

Dale swung and swung and swung some more. His mouth was open, lips curled back over his teeth, and he realized he was screaming. Guttural. Primal. A roar as his arms swung madly. Mercer backed into a wall, head teetering woozily on his neck, the wall the only thing holding him up. His ugly face was bloody and contused. Dale felt the anger in him as he grabbed Mercer's shirt, and he envisioned the next blow, straight to the man's face. Dale's fist went back, tightened, and—

He stopped.

Despite his lofty ideas about hate and the power that

good had over evil, for last few moments, Dale had been filled with nothing but hate as he'd swung mercilessly at Mercer. He'd let his emotions rule, and if he went any further—

A sharp pain to Dale's side.

Piercing, blinding pain. Right below his ribs.

Dale's vision flashed white, and a wave of cool sweat swept over his forehead. He looked down. Mercer's hand, pressed against him. The handle of a switchblade up to Dale's side, below his ribs. All the way to the hilt.

Dale's eyes looked up and met those of Mercer. They were bloodied, beaten. But they twinkled. And a smile came to his lips.

Another bolt of searing pain. Mercer had yanked the blade out.

Dale stumbled backwards. He was bent over. There was a moment where Mercer stayed reclined against the wall, gathering his strength, summoning his reserves. Then he slowly stood up. Stretched out to his full, long length. He took a deep breath, twisted his neck to the left and right, popping it.

And then he stepped toward Dale.

A kick with one of his long legs. Dale was still bent over, and the kick caught him in the chest. This pushed Dale back farther. His feet shuffled on the cement. He barely maintained balance.

Mercer came forward. An uppercut, catching Dale right where he'd been stabbed. Dale screamed. He was still hunched. Mercer grabbed his hair, yanked, and punched the wound again. And again.

Huge, terrible waves of pain surged through Dale. He tried to shield the wound with his arm, but the punches came, over and over. Fast. Dale's vision grew lighter. The sounds of the waves began to fade.

The blows were pushing him backward, farther and farther, his feet shuffling against the cement, and Mercer

followed, swinging those arms. Dale remembered how he had
been punching Mercer relentlessly, like the man was doing to
him now. The hate that Dale had felt. He had let himself go.
And now the tables had turned on him.

Mercer reared back and let another huge punch go. Dale's
senses were so muted that it hardly hurt.

The blow knocked him over. He landed against the opposite wall.

Dale shook his head. Woozy. He was lying in a pile of junk
from the construction. A couple partial bags of cement. A
few pieces of rebar. Mercer was a few feet in front of him,
silhouetted against one of the windows behind him. He
stepped forward and inverted the knife in his hand, put it in a
stabbing position, like *Psycho*. Dale watched his own blood
dripping off the blade, glistening in the moonlight

"This is where it ends for you, Special Agent Dale
Conley."

This was *not* where it ended.

Dale's vision was lightening rapidly, but even in his
current state he knew that there was always an answer. Everything works out if you give it time, and he still had a few
seconds before Mercer would be upon him.

Something was brushing up against his hand. He glanced,
askance. It was a piece of rebar. Short. A trimming. About a
foot and a half long. Sheared to a shiny, pointy end.

Perfect.

As Mercer moved toward him, Dale targeted exactly
where he would need to pierce him with the rebar. He was
going to have to kill the man. It was him or Dale. Straight
into the chest. He could angle it up and jab slightly to the left
when Mercer was about two feet away.

Mercer lumbered forward. He smiled. The knife looked
gigantic.

Dale slid his fingers toward the rebar.

He took a big breath. He needed every bit of his remaining energy to do this. He'd have to spring up, quickly.

He watched Mercer's feet.

Just come forward two more steps.

Then Dale would jab, at a forty-five-degree angle.

Mercer took another step.

Come on. Come on. I can handle you. I got this.

Dale wrapped his fingers around the rebar. The time was now. He tensed his legs.

Angle this just right.

Mercer's foot lifted off the floor.

Dale put his other hand flat, ready to push off, to spring to his feet. Now all he needed to do was—

Mercer stopped moving. His eyes went wide. And he jolted. Something came out of his chest. Something small and round, dark. Rebar. His mouth opened. He coughed.

Was Dale delirious? Had he done it?

Dale was still on the floor. He looked down. His fingers were wrapped around the rebar, the sheared tip resting beside his thigh. He looked back at Mercer.

The rebar coming from his chest moved, shoved out another few inches. Blood oozed down to the tip, dripped off. There was another sputter from Mercer's lips, and he dropped to his knees.

Luanne stood behind him.

Her hands were in front of her chest, one in front of the other, still in the position they'd been when she'd shoved the piece of metal through her husband's back. She quivered, and her eyes were wide and dilated. Mental shock.

Blood came out of Mercer's mouth. Bubbly. Frothy. His body fell forward, landing a foot in front of Dale, facedown. The rebar *clanked* against the cement.

Luanne was frozen, her eyes still staring into nothing, shaking.

Dale used that bit of energy he'd been reserving for the attack and stood up, hobbled over to her, put a hand on her shoulder.

"What have I done?" she said. "Oh my god. What have I done?"

"I was in mortal danger. You came to the aid of a federal agent," he said and put his hands on her face, turned it to look at him. Her eyes avoided his. "You've done a good thing here, Luanne."

"But ... but ... What will happen now? My boys ... The men in his group. They'll come for us."

He took both of her hands in his. "Listen to me, Luanne."

She looked at him. He'd gotten her attention.

"The organization I work for, we make things happen," he said. "We can protect you. Every resource is available to you. We can make you disappear. From this day forward, you have not a thing to worry about."

Her eyes moved briefly to Mercer's body and back to him. Then she took in a deep breath.

"Now ... could I get a ride to the hospital?"

CHAPTER FIFTY-TWO

IT WAS STILL early in the morning, and the Grizzly took a final look at the front page of *The Times-Picayune* before placing it on the chessboard surface of his desk. The top headline read: *Gulf-Wide Task Force Diverts Potential Drug Disaster.* And the byline read: *Notorious Figure Jesse James Killed on Bourbon Street.*

It was a stranger end to things than he would have expected. A very unorthodox endgame. But it was an ending. The Grizzly had in no way tried to be a hero when he spread the word that the tainted drugs were going to be mass-released. Still, he felt sort of good about it. In a fashion, he'd help stop a tragedy. This made him think of the two federal agents and their passion.

It also made him think of the repercussions that would come from abusing the agents' trust.

There was a knock at his door.

"Yes?"

Rhino walked in. A small piece of paper was in his hand. "You got a telegram."

"A ... telegram?"

The Grizzly took the note.

Checkmate, Grizzly.
Dale Conley
😊♡

Dale Conley. The agent from the DOJ.

Clever. But what could it mean?

The Grizzly's perpetual smile broadened a bit.

There was a burst of noise from the other side of his door, coming from the club. Shouts, banging.

He looked at Rhino. "Check it."

As Rhino stepped away, the Grizzly glanced at the note. He shook his head.

Before Rhino could leave the room, the door swung open and cracked into the wall loudly.

"Federal agents! Hands in the air!"

Four people burst into his office. Three men and a woman. All waving guns. All wearing sunglasses. All with jackets bearing the letters DEA.

The Grizzly admired cunning, cleverness, a perfectly-timed move. From his smile, the low rumble of a laugh started. A little chuckle.

The DEA agents spread out into the room. Screaming. One of them went toward Rhino. Another couple headed his way.

He raised his hands, stood up. And laughed louder.

CHAPTER FIFTY-THREE

IT WAS PUSHING LUNCHTIME, but still Dale had a cup of coffee between his hands as he looked out to the water. After all the festivities with Dylan Mercer last night, he'd taken a trip to the hospital and handled a barrage of paperwork. With only a smidgen of sleep, he'd made the three-hour drive to Pensacola for this meeting.

The message had instructed him to meet outside the Pensacola Municipal Auditorium. It was a huge structure, and surrounding it was a drive and a wide walkway going up to the water of Pensacola Bay. The sky was bright blue with only a couple small clouds. The air was calm, and sunlight sparkled off the gentle waves. It was a very public location, people all around. This was why Dale thought it safe to meet with the man.

Dale took another sip of coffee and saw someone approaching. The man was on the short side, about five-foot-seven, in his sixties, round cheeks on a kind-looking face with twinkling eyes. He looked a bit like a de-aged and clean-shaven Santa Claus, but if this man was associated with the group he claimed to be, there was nothing sweet about him.

Dale faced him. "Mick Henderson?"

The man nodded and stopped a few feet away from Dale. "That's right." He had a thick Southern accent.

"Got your note, Mick. But it was a little light on the details. It just said that you can tell me about the Knights of the Golden Circle."

Henderson smiled. "I can, but first I want you to know that this is all entirely off the record. I need to make sure you're not wearing a wire." He held up his hands and gave him a little look that said, *Do you mind?*

Dale sighed. "You serious? Fine."

Dale grabbed his gun and holster from the back of his jeans then raised his arms and let Henderson pat him down. When Henderson got close to his crotch, this was usually the time when Dale would crack some sort of smartass joke. But he kept reminding himself that this man claimed to be part of an organization devoted to slavery in the modern world. Dale wasn't in a joking mood.

Henderson finished.

"Satisfied?" Dale said. "Now tell me, why are you offering me information?"

Henderson handed him a folder. "I'm giving you information on the Second KGC, Dylan Mercer's fraudulent KGC. In there you'll find the names of every knight."

Dale nodded. He looked at the folder but didn't open it. "And what about your real KGC?"

"The way I figure, you must be part of some covert agency, looking into societies like us. Certainly Luanne Mercer told you what happened before you arrived at Pensacola Beach last night. There's no use in denying we exist. But I want you to know that you shouldn't be wasting your time trying to find us." He paused. "But you're going to, aren't you?"

Dale nodded. "Of course I am. I'll be looking for you."

Henderson shook his head. "Boy, we've been in the shadows for over a hundred years. We are a *secret* society, after all."

He smiled then turned and walked away.

CHAPTER FIFTY-FOUR

BACK IN NEW ORLEANS, the sky was still bright, and the sun was hot. Dale stood on the sidewalk along Rampart Street outside the police station. He was with Allie. A taxi sat at the end of the block, idling.

Allie was wearing sunglasses, and she took them off to look at him, squinting a little as she adjusted to the sunlight. Dale took his off too.

"This was something else," Allie said, shaking her head. "Life's always exciting with you."

She put out her hand, and Dale took it.

He mustered up a cheeseball voice, something like a sports announcer or a radio DJ. "Well, I am a man of mystery and intrigue."

Allie rolled her eyes. She took her hand back and adjusted her purse.

"This is obviously a moot point," Dale said, "but can I get your number?"

Allie shook her head. "No."

Dale's heart jumped. "What are you talking about?"

"Some things are best left where they were, Dale."

Panic. This wasn't real. She was playing a cruel joke on him.

"But ... last night."

"Last night was what it was." Her voice was flat. Impersonal. She wasn't joking.

For once, Dale was completely speechless. A thousand thoughts rushed to him. The idea of a future with Allie. The image he'd made, based on the feeling they'd shared, the assurance that she'd given to him with her look and words and passion and holding his hand. She'd held his hand in the car. In just a couple days, he'd unburied a feeling that had been hidden for years, brought it back up and made it most important, made it as important as it should've been in the first place. And he'd developed a plan. A loose plan, perhaps, but a plan. An idea for a future.

Dale tried to speak. All that came out were pitiful beginnings. "But ... I ... But..."

Allie looked down at the taxi on the corner, put her sunglasses on, and turned back to him. "I gotta go, Dale."

Dale was the sort of man who took action, and taking action leads one to getting what one wants. His brain couldn't reconcile what was happening. He'd taken action, but he couldn't get what he wanted. Another person's will was at odds with it.

"So, this was nothing?"

"Like I said, it was what it was." She sighed. "I gotta go."

"No," Dale said.

He was always a master of words, a skilled communicator, but the only word that kept flashing across his mind was *No*.

No.

She turned.

"Baby, no."

"I'm not your baby, Dale."

"Last night we said—"

"Everybody says 'baby' during that."

Ouch. Ouch indeed.

She started walking away.

Dale followed.

"No."

He grabbed her arm.

She stopped. Her eyes went to his hand

"Don't grab me, Dale."

Dale's mind flashed back to the wounds on Luanne Mercer. Physical dominance. He didn't want Allie to feel even a tiny fraction of that. He quickly pulled his hand away

She started toward the taxi again. He followed after her.

"Allie."

She kept walking.

He stopped. She continued. He saw just her back and her red hair shining in the sun. Distance grew between them.

"Allison."

She didn't stop. A few feet farther away.

"Al!"

Allie whipped around, stomped back toward him. "*What, Dale? What?*"

He was panting, and he breathed in twice before he said it.

"I love you."

There was a pause. She slowly put her hand to her sunglasses and removed them again. She looked up at him. "Oh, Dale." She put her hand on his cheek. "Dale, Dale, Dale." Her eyes moved left and right across his. "You don't know how to love."

She turned around again and walked away. As she did, she put her sunglasses back on. Dale stood where he was.

It was different than the first time, years ago, when he asked her if she ever wanted to see him again, and she said no. That had been at night. And cold. And when he stepped out of her apartment, it was raining. Back then, he hadn't known what to make of his feelings for her. He hadn't been the man he was now. This time, it was sunny and bright. His skin was wet with sweat not dappled with rain. And it wasn't him walking away from her. He was watching as she walked away from him. To the taxi.

Her freckled arm reaching out for the door handle.

The last glimpse of her red hair.

Her long legs slipping in.

The car door shutting.

Dale's future changed again. It had shifted, momentarily, to something new and fulfilling. And now it had shifted back in the direction it had been—yet onto a different path entirely. The path he'd been on before he began this assignment in New Orleans had its fair share of scars, and one of those scars was Allie. This new path had a gaping wound. And something told Dale it would never completely scar over.

The taxi's turn signal came on, and it pulled onto Rampart Street.

Dale had been thinking a lot about love during this assignment. Love as compared to hate. But the word *love* had many different meanings, one of those being romantic love. While he watched the taxi, a suspicion Dale had was confirmed. Romantic love was not real. It was a transmutation of physical intimacy. Lust. The idea of a romantic, cosmic connection with a person was merely an extension of sex.

Like a love scene in a movie. Why was a sex scene called a "love" scene? A love scene should be a grandfather passing on a meaningful heirloom to a young boy, a woman burying the dog that had been her faithful companion for twelve years—not two lustful drunks stumbling home from a bar to make an even trade of gonorrhea for chlamydia.

A love scene.

That's all he'd had with Allie. Their love scene.

One scene.

Anger rose in him. Almost hatred.

Yes, the idea of romantic love was a crock of shit. And not fresh, steaming shit. Oh no. Putrid, old shit, crusted over on the top. Two lonely flies languidly buzzing around it. Ancient flies on the twenty-seventh day of their twenty-eight-day lifespan, realizing that even they could do no better.

An overflowing crock of horse shit.

The taxi was almost out of sight now. He saw it take a right. It went around a corner. And then it was gone.

Complete and utter horse shit.

For some reason Dale thought about Percy and Bonita.

Okay, maybe there were a few exceptions. Just a few.

He wondered how far the taxi had gotten. It had turned onto Conti Street, so maybe if he ran down to Basin he might be able to see it as it—

He stopped himself. This was pathetic. The great Dale Conley was being pathetic. He had always been one for quick and immediate adaptation, so he needed to come to a realization and fast: Allie was gone.

He felt his eyes grow tight, warm, moist.

He opened them wide, tilted his head back, tried to keep everything in. His sunglasses were still off. The sky was bright.

During assignments, Dale always managed to keep his thoughts focused, but the amount of data in his brain could be an overwhelming whirlwind, and at times like this, it bombarded him with factual information, things of reason to dull an emotion that was overtaking him.

The Greeks. Athenians. They had ideas on romantic love. Theories, presented in Plato's *Symposium*. When they were giving speeches about the deity Eros, one of six people stated that—

There was a voice behind him. Percy. "Hey there."

Footsteps. Percy was approaching.

Of course, Freud was a significant factor in the theories of romance in the twentieth century. His idea of the family drama. But there were others who had their own ideas. René Girard, for one, thought—

Percy stepped up beside him. "Allie gone? Dang, I'd hoped to have a chance to say goodbye."

Dale didn't acknowledge him, just continued to tilt his head back and look at the sky.

Percy leaned closer. "Hey, are you … are you crying, man?" There was a teasing tone in his voice.

"No," Dale said.

"Yes, you are."

Dale put his sunglasses on. "It doesn't count if nothing comes out."

There was a pause as Percy thought things through. "Wait a minute, did you and Allie …? You old dog!" Percy smacked his back.

Dale still didn't look at him. He turned farther way. He was embarrassed.

"Ohhhh…" Percy said, and his tone got much more serious. "Oh, I see what's going on here. She's gone, huh?"

Dale didn't answer. He felt Percy's hand on his shoulder.

"Oh, Dale. I'm so sorry." Percy stepped in front of him, trying to get in his line of vision.

Cleopatra and Mark Antony. Edward and Wallis. Napoleon and Josephine. Napoleon divorced her when she couldn't have children. He wanted an heir. Henry VIII made the same sort of decision three hundred years earlier, creating an *entire church* to serve—

"Dale…"

Ancient mythology. The Trojan War had started because

of love. Helen, the face that launched a thousand ships. And Paris, who—

"Dale, come on." Percy raised out his arms, fluttered his fingers as though inviting Dale in for a hug. "Come here."

Dale didn't budge.

Percy continued with his finger movements. "Come on. Dock it in at Hug Harbor, big guy."

Dale conceded, stepped forward, and hugged his friend.

CHAPTER FIFTY-FIVE

WHENEVER ONE OF SAC Walter Taft's BEI agents went through a major personal dilemma, he offered to "buy them a dog." Not a puppy. A hotdog. From the stand a couple blocks away from the BEI office in D.C.

This was the second time Taft had done this for Dale, the first time being when Dale's mother had landed in critical care at the hospital. It was an odd gift for Taft to give to Dale since the man was well aware of Dale's healthy eating habits, but it was a nice gesture nonetheless. One hotdog wouldn't kill Dale.

It was a warm day, but it felt cool and comfortable after spending so much time in the muggy Gulf South. Dale had been back in D.C. for two days. As he strolled down Constitution Avenue—with the traffic flowing steadily beside him; car horns and engines—Dale saw that Taft was not alone at the hotdog stand. Behind him was Arty Marty, who was clad entirely in dark blue.

At the sidewalk on the other side of the street was a painter. A woman. She sat on a folding chair behind an easel and was painting the streetscape in front of her. Around her were several paintings that she was selling, propped against the small wall bordering the lawn of the National Museum of Natural History behind her. She sat in the shade of the big trees growing in the museum's lawn. Her hair was dark brown and straight, and her face was heart-shaped. She made eye contact with him. Held the gaze for moment. Then returned to her painting.

Dale stepped up to the hotdog stand. "Hey-a, sir."

Taft grunted.

"Arty Marty, how are ya?"

Marty scowled at his nickname. "I'm fine, Dale. Thank you."

Dale glanced over his associate's clothes. "What period are we in now, Marty? Navy blue?"

"Indigo, Dale. Are you blind?"

"My mistake."

Taft handed Dale a hotdog.

"Thank you, sir."

Dale looked at the dog in his hand. He remembered some footage he'd seen on TV—the making of hotdogs. They were made from a slurry.

A slurry.

Taft grabbed a yellow plastic bottle and squeezed mustard onto his hotdog. "Percy Gordon's wrapping up all the loose ends. Another week or so, he said. Then he's off to Houston. Did you say your goodbyes? I know you two are pals."

"We did."

It had been another bit of sadness at the end of the assignment when Dale had bid Percy farewell. They gave each another brief hug. Not the same kind of hug as the one that came after Allie had plunged her little hand into Dale's sternum and ripped out his still-beating heart, but it was good nonetheless. It said what it needed to.

"So you've got something for me in Milwaukee?" Dale said.

"Yes, I do," Taft said and shook a manila folder he had in his hand. He took a big bite of hotdog, chewed it, then continued talking with his mouth full. "But I'm thinking of offering you a couple days off."

"Are you feeling all right, sir?"

"Gordon told me what happened with Al, Conley. Why do you think I'm buying you the damn hotdog? Do you need some time to think things through, get your head on straight?"

Dale thought this over for a moment. He looked across the street. The painter. She was looking his way. She smiled. He smiled back then checked her left hand. No wedding ring, unlike the last girl who'd given him a smile at the café in New Orleans.

He turned back to Taft. "I'm fine, sir. What's going on in Milwaukee?" He reached for the folder.

Taft glanced over at the painter and back to Dale. A grin came to Taft's lips. Dale was floored. A Walter Taft smile was rarer than most of the fossils in the nearby museum.

"Glad to have you back, Conley." He tightened his grip on the folder, wouldn't let Dale take it. "You're sure?"

Dale nodded and tugged the folder out of Taft's hand. "Why would I need time off?" He opened the folder, flipped through the contents. A crime scene photo. A copy of a note in Victorian-era handwriting. A list of numbers. Dale's heartbeat quickened. "After all, I love this job."

ALSO BY ERIK CARTER

ACKNOWLEDGMENTS

For their involvement with *The Lowdown*, I would like to give a sincere thank you to:

My ARC readers, for providing reviews and catching typos. Thanks!

Dad, for answering numerous questions about police work and those groovy '70s.

Mom, for sharing some technical expertise.

April Snellings, for editorial assistance with the first few chapters—amazing, as always.

Jacki Wilson at the UWF Historic Trust, for her resources and personal knowledge.

Mike Thomin, my history buddy, for tracking down some research sources.

My friends and family, for the support.